We reached the garage safely.

The Embassy—not quite.

The chauffeur swung the car into the garage—the self-opening doors going shut behind us—and over to a recharge post at the far end. As usual, he turned the car round and backed in so that the rear fender just nudged the recharge post as the car stopped.

And the damn thing exploded.

It wasn't an accident; there is no way in the world for an electric auto-recharge post to explode in the course of nature. Someone had booby-trapped the thing . . . and it sprayed bits of itself all over the garage.

Most of the pieces fell on other cars, landed in the walls, bounded off the metal of our car. One piece—long, thin and sharp—came straight through the rear window and into the back of Pollorine's head.

He was dead before he could make a sound.

When the game gets very serious, it's best to keep a

Knave in Hand

Laurence M. Janifer hasn't changed much this year. The same specs listed in his first Knave novel (SURVIVOR, August 1977) are still around to be applied. He is one year older, and that's about it.

He has written some more stories, and many more letters. He is now often found smoking a pipe, on medical instructions that baffle the Hell out of him. Knave is still smoking those Inoson things.

A few of Knave's shorter adventures have popped up in ROM, of all places. ROM is a magazine for computer people. Others—and doubtless some more long ones—will be appearing here and there, as soon as Mr. Janifer hears about them from Knave.

Neither Mr. Janifer nor Knave understands the way Tocks live, or the way they think. If either of them ever digs up any more information, or a theory of Tock behavior that will stand in a high wind, the news will become generally available, one way or another. The possibility seems awfully remote, though.

Knave in Hand

by

Laurence M. Janifer

SF
ace books

A Division of Charter Communications Inc.
A GROSSET & DUNLAP COMPANY
360 Park Avenue South
New York, New York 10010

KNAVE IN HAND

An ACE Book

First Ace printing: March 1979

Printed in U.S.A.

Let's put it another way.

If anybody gets the notion that he is meant to resemble some character, or for all I know tree, building or couch, in this book, it seems reasonable to ask him to wait until the date in which the events in this book take place before coming round with a subpoena in his hand. That date is approximately 2300 A.D.; the subpoena will still be procured on a wrong assumption, since all these people here are themselves, and not resemblances of other people, but at least it will be appropriately timed.

And, once again, the opinions of Gerald Knave do not necessarily reflect those of the author. Nine times out of ten, maybe, but no better than that. In fact, this book is not a reflecting-pool: it is a book. I hope that is all right with everybody.

This is to celebrate
Amy and Freff,
Kelly and Polly,
and especially Trina and Peter Lancaster,
who might all be shining models
of Nassanank and Jessiss.

PROLOGUE

The human race has developed a variety of theories regarding social systems. The Tocks have never had a theory at all. The Tocks have never needed one: they live in a social system that works, and have about as much use for pure theory as human beings have for a Theory of Breathing.

They have a name for their world, which human beings have never been able to pronounce; we call it Haven IV, and it is a little too cold for comfortable human habitation. Luckily—for the Tocks, or for human beings, it's hard to be sure —Haven IV is part of a very unusual system, one in which there are three possible planets for colonization. Human beings settled Haven II and Haven III long ago, and live their own lives there; on Haven IV there are always a few tourists, a Consular representative handling Tock-human affairs, a fully staffed Embassy, a military cadre that doubles as police force—human beings need a police force: Tocks very nearly don't, and the entire planet is patrolled by perhaps seventy-five Tock policemen—and a small human colony. Some of the people in that colony are there on business, of one or another long-term sort: there is a little Tock-human trade, mostly inside the Haven system and mostly in foods and spices; there are some Socioeconomic Statics researchers, every one of whom has taken the least interesting thing on Haven IV to survey: the social system of the Tocks.

There are others, of course; where humans settle, there always will be. There are suppliers and shopkeepers to the military and diplomatic departments; there are grocers, bakers, innkeepers, shoe repairmen and so forth for the human colony as a whole. Like any isolated colony, the one on Haven IV has become almost a small world of its own, not quite self-sustaining but close to it.

And then there are a few people who just happen to like very cold weather, and who also happen to like snakes—which is what the Tocks seem most to resemble.

They are not exactly snakes; parallel evolution is one of those notions that looks plausible only from a distance, and only preSpace. They have legs like lizards—short and thick—and the legs fold up into the body and can be covered by hard flaps, so a Tock can either walk or wiggle as it happens to suit him. (Or her: the Tocks have two sexes—two and a half, really, but the Media are seldom seen by human beings, seldom spoken of by Tocks.) It averages out to about sixty or seventy legs per Tock; there is no strict number, any more than there's a strict number for the hairs on your head. Some Tocks are sparsely legged, comparatively speaking, and some have a full, fine growth.

The analogy stops at that point: Tocks don't go bald. That is: a) their feet don't fall off, and b) they have no hair anywhere to worry about. They are not truly exoskeletal, but they look it: a Tock, fully flapped in, has a shiny, hard skin that looks like a carapace.

Humans discovered them—to begin with—before Haven II and Haven III were settled. The unmanned Exploration Ships noted all three worlds as possible settlements, reported back the total lack of intelligent life on the inner two planets, and evidence of an indigenous race of high intelligence on the outer one.

That particular Exploration Ship never landed on Haven IV: in accordance with the taped instructions it had carried through space-four all the way from the Home Worlds, it became a UFO. It did its best to be inconspicuous, staying a long way above the balance limit of 19,800 miles. (Haven IV gravitation is slightly less than Earth normal; Haven II is 1.03 Earth normal, Haven III is .96 Earth normal. As stated, an unusual system—there are astronomical theorists who call it impossible, but the planets don't seem to mind). It hung in darkness, radiating nothing whatever in any way detectable out of space-four, and the Tocks took a full four days to find out it was up there.

They did not attempt to blow it up. They did not begin cautious negotiations with it.

They invited it down, for a landing.

The Tock social system works. They assume, until clearly informed otherwise, that all social systems work.

Conflict is a rare occurrence, studiable in learned Tock periodicals (or equivalent) under names like Fiss Syndrome and Wenspiss Disruptive Disease.

The Exploration Ship didn't land, or reply. It had no instructions in the matter, which for even a sophisticated computer is the exact equivalent of the statement: This matter does not exist.

It waited.

The first colonists came to Haven III. The second wave came to Haven II.

The third wave settled on III and, cautiously, slowly, every probe out and every system on alert, made overtures toward Haven IV.

The Tocks, by that time, had learned human language: Comity Standard, with a Tock accent that consists mostly of hisses. They had the broadcasts going on throughout both the inner planets to work with, and the Tocks are a highly intelligent species.

They replied to the overtures with another invitation: "Come and see for yourselves. Delighted to have you, stay as long as you like."

That sort of thing.

The human race is not at all used to that sort of thing.

Cautiously, however, it responded to the invitation. A few human beings traveled by ordinary boost from Haven III to a hastily cleared area which the Tocks christened a spaceport (and have since built up into a very lavish display). They spoke with the leaders of the Tocks; they traded the equivalent of beads and baubles; they discussed diplomatic relations.

Diplomatic relations surprised the Tocks, when they began to understand what had been meant. But their monitoring of the Haven II and III broadcasts had begun to give them a background; they were slowly coming to realize that they were dealing with an entire race that was down with Fiss Syndrome and Wenspiss Disruptive Disease.

If you can't cure them, humor them; that seems to be the Tock attitude. They set up the proper diplomatic structures, found an Ambassador and a staff—they were excused from maintaining actual residence on an inner planet, of course; the Tocks know a good deal about space travel, at least of the boost variety, but they have never set feet, so to speak, off Haven IV, and they never will. They don't like the idea; an absolute reluctance seems to be built in.

Whether this reluctance has anything to do with the fact that they have a social system that really, honestly, totally works—that, as they say, is an interesting question. You can find arguments on both sides in the learned journals, and you can find arguments on sides you never dreamed existed.

The Tocks themselves neither know nor care; that's the way things are, and that's the way they always have been.

After nearly a hundred years of study and argument, the one thing on which human beings and Tocks are absolutely agreed is: the Tock social system works beautifully—for Tocks. Transplanting it to humanity would be a very quick way to cause a disaster; though God knows it's tempting to try. I understand that some Frontier Planet group did actually take a Socioeconomic Statics text on the Tock social system as a sort of Bible and made a grand attempt to live by it.

There don't seem to have been any results. That particular group—unless the whole thing is baseless rumor, which is just barely possible—left no survivors.

The Tocks have a sort of Absolute Monarchy (King, Queen and Chief Medium, more or less; the Queen's official title translates as "egg-warmer and main twiner," if you want precision) tempered by chaos. The King and Queen rule, serve as interpreters-of-last-resort for all Tock law and custom, and have every imaginable power over the race. Every nine days, this is not true at all.

A sort of constant lottery is taking place. (How this is managed nobody knows; there are theories that telepathy enters into it, and there are other theories that sound even less likely.) Every nine days some Tock is chosen—by pure chance—as King (or Queen). And for that day, his rule is absolute; if he feels like it he can order half the Tocks to murder the other half, and, as far as anyone has ever been able to see (and as the Tocks clearly state), he would be obeyed. Some of these Kings-by-chance have ordered even odder things—and the race has obeyed.

(The Media don't get into this much. They're the extra sex, or half-sex; they are not intelligent by any test either Tock or human has ever been able to devise, and they are treated more like pets than anything else. A given male Tock may board a Medium, feed and water it and take it for walks, until he meets a female Tock who accepts what amounts to his proposal of marriage —joint ownership of the Medium. It can go the other way, too, and does just as often: a female Tock boards a Medium, and proposes to a male. There is a marked male-female difference among Tocks—easily as marked as that among human beings—but it doesn't seem to express itself in either direction as far as a Medium is concerned.)

When the chance day is over, the reigning King and Queen take back the reins, restore order where necessary, and go right on as if nothing had happened. Nine days later. . .

You get the idea. For Tocks, it works; and Tocks are not human beings. It's a little like staring into a mirror and seeing yourself with an extra nose sticking out of the top of your head. They act human—almost. You feel you can understand them. Everything makes perfect sense.

But what in Hell is that nose doing up there?

Suppose (for instance) that the Comity were ruled by this sort of absolute-monarch King and Queen; and suppose someone actually managed the job every thief, in every monarchy, has dreamed about at least once in his career.

Suppose the Crown Jewels were stolen.

The Tocks did have Crown Jewels—but it wasn't a crown, and they weren't jewels. And they did have a small number of anti-social acts —that's what their seventy-five-person police force was for, mostly.

Imagine the hue and cry! Imagine the excitement, the rumors, the rushing back and forth, the attempts to get the jewels out of the vicinity in order to deposit them with a trusted fence—

Imagine, in short, everything that didn't happen.

The Tock Crown Jewels actually were stolen. And you haven't heard a word about it, not over the 3V, not in the papers—because human beings hushed up the affair.

Not Tocks.

They didn't do any hushing; it wouldn't occur to them. They didn't do any frenzied talking, either.

They—the King and Queen and the Royal Household, which was and is extensive and puzzling—waited two weeks, "in order," as the King, Nassanank, said later, "to be sure it was not an inadvertence"—in order, as far as that makes any sense, to make certain somebody hadn't just wandered off with the stuff by accident, and would be along to return it as soon as he came to his senses.

Then they got in touch with the Consular officials, and the whole damned Embassy on Haven IV—the official representatives of the human race.

The Embassy and Consulate—why are there both? Because one is from Haven II and one is from Haven III; Haven II has the Embassy, and most of the representation. They conferred together, got in touch with several experts in Socioeconomic Statics who had done books on the Tocks, and conferred some more. All this took time—three to four weeks.

The Tocks displayed no impatience. "What a person mars, he cures," Nassanank told the Ambassador at some point during all of this. "We assume that the same is true of races."

Nassanank was sure, in other words, that we'd taken the jewels—and that we'd get them back.

The trouble was that the jewels—well, they had no value except as curios, off Haven IV. They were a great array of globules arranged in an uneven spiral. Every globule was three-quarters filled with water. In each globule a fish lived. The fish—it's a rare species on Haven IV, always known as the King's Gift and not kept in private hands; if a fisher gets one in his net he turns it over to the treasury, which credits him with available work-days so that he doesn't have to retire as soon as usual—the fish lives in its little habitat, which is a balanced ecosystem, believe it or not.

And the fish lights up.

Every one is a slightly different color, or combination of colors. And the lighting is intermittent throughout the life of the fish (which is measurable in hundreds of years).

The effect is something awesome.

But who'd want to steal them? Off Haven IV they might have had some curio value, but "unmarketable" isn't the word for that spiral, or its component parts; no fence in the known Galaxy would touch it. The King's Gift belongs on Haven IV, and everybody knows it, and one found elsewhere would create a Diplomatic Incident, which would lead to—well, nobody knows what.

And nobody wants to find out.

The Comity has a damned long arm, if the reach is worth the trouble. It would have reached for anybody who tried to market so much as a single fish off Haven IV, and everybody knew that, too.

Haven IV—the Tocks—don't have any fences. They might turn up a jewel thief once a century or so; but what would even he do with the Crown Jewels?

But they had undeniably been stolen.

It was an interesting puzzle. Who had stolen an immensely valuable item nobody wanted?

As I say, the human contingent on Haven IV conferred, off and on, for four weeks. Then somebody made the obvious suggestion—I suppose it was obvious—and everyone instantly agreed.

They called me. *Gerald Knave: Survivor,* as it says on my cards.

I got the call just before people started getting killed.

CHAPTER ONE

There was a lot of loose talk about a reward. I stamped that out as fast as I could—within hours of landing on Haven IV, in fact.

I came down in my own ship—it's a one-man job, with facilities for a few guests, and it looks quite innocent and is slightly less heavily armed than a Comity starship—and parked where they told me to park, waited for the radiation-proof ramp to come wheeling by (there's always residual radiation when you land on a planet; you may make a close approach through space-four, but the last bit has to be done on boost), and stepped onto it when it did. After all those weeks of discussion, the Consulate and Embassy were a surprisingly impatient group of people; there were three of them on the ramp when I got onto it.

One—a tall, lanky woman with a face like a very well-bred horse—said: "Knave? We don't want you wasting any time on this. It's an important job."

The man next to her—slightly shorter, slightly fatter, a few wisps of white hair and the expression of a benevolent uncle—said quietly:

"You must excuse us. We're quite upset by all this."

I looked at the third arrival (medium height, rounder than usual, a bowler hat and a waxed moustache). His contribution was: "Of course you understand, Knave. And we do want results in a hurry—need them, in fact. We're offering quite a sizable reward—"

By that time the ramp had parked itself in the slot of the Embarcation Building, and they were blocking my way off. The first view of that building from just inside—at the top of the ramp, sixty feet in the air and perhaps half a mile from the center of the great circle—is enough to stop anybody, any time. A lot of the wall material is quartz, or a local equivalent, and the building glitters all over. Down below are the swarms of people heading here, there and everywhere—occasionally a Tock, perhaps to see someone off or meet an arrival, never to go off on his own—and the shop-buildings and travelers' aids—all housed in the one immense dome of quartz, but every one a different size, a different shape, a different shade—all solid colors, smooth concrete. Around us were other ramps; above us was the top of the dome—I don't know any process that allows that big a free curve of stained glass, but the top of the Haven IV dome is just that, an immense cap of colors, abstract, so that the light into the place is in shafts of red, blue, yellow— everything you can think of, and all of it reflecting off the quartz, off the polished floor, off the solid-color small buildings and the ramps. . . .

I wouldn't want to live there—too damned

cold—but it is one Hell of a place to visit.

"No reward," I said, after a while. I'm not sure how long a while.

The man in the bowler said: "But, Knave—"

"No reward," I said again. "I'm for hire, and I get a lot of work because I do a useful job: I survive. It's the only profession I know of, theological considerations aside, that's defensible as important. The only one."

The horse-faced woman said: "Now, really—"

"At any rate," I said, "it's important to you, or I wouldn't be here. I'm an expert on survival —and maybe I can help you people survive whatever catastrophe you've had fall in on you. But I'm not going into it on the basis of a reward. I want payment—flat fee or percentage, we can discuss it when I know what the problem is. But payment—success or failure, glory, death or doom."

There was a little silence. The horse-faced woman said: "That strikes me as—as an incredibly arrogant attitude. After all—"

"It isn't an attitude," I said. "It's a business. *Gerald Knave: Survivor*—remember? And insisting on terms like that is one of the ways by which I survive."

The short man—the quiet type—couldn't help it. He began to chuckle. The horse-faced woman shot him a glare that should, by rights, have melted his head.

"We'll discuss this—demand—later," she said to me.

"We'll discuss it now," I said, "or I will, by God, ride this damned ramp right on back to my ship, unseal, send back the ramp and leave for a civilized planet."

Nobody ever wants to pay the piper, pied or otherwise. Actually, I think I got away with a little less speechmaking than usual; we were settled that I was going in on a flat fee, win, lose or draw, before they stepped aside and I opened the ramp door and we all went down the steps into chaos.

Chaos was a tall, ridiculously thin man in a checked jumper, coming across that gleaming floor toward us and waving a piece of paper. "Mr. Benson!" he was shouting as he got closer. "Mr. Benson, please—wait—"

We stopped in a body. The tall man shot past several startled groups of businessmen, tourists or experts, reached us and came to a skidding halt. He gulped for breath.

My benevolent uncle said: "Yes, Timmins?"

"Mr. Benson—" He didn't quite have his breath back, but he was in no mood to wait for it. "Mr. Benson—this just came in—I drove over here—hoped to catch you before you met—"

"We have already met Mr. Knave," Benson said, just as mildly as ever. "Now: what's this that's just 'come over'? Come over what?"

"News wire," Timmins gasped. "Not on the 3V yet—will be in an hour or two. No way to keep it quiet—and God knows what it means, but—part of the problem, and you ought to know it before you give orders—to Mr. Knave—"

People do not, in fact, give orders to Mr. Knave; but it wasn't worth discussion just then.

The original call had given me very little background—something vital had been stolen for no reason anybody could figure out, and it had to be got back—but maybe, I thought, the little piece of paper would give me some more. I reached for it.

Benson was ahead of me. He was still very gentle and very quiet as he read the thing, looked up at all of us, and said: "General Tal has just been assassinated."

The horse-faced woman said: "Oh, my God."

The man in the bowler said: "Exactly, Betty, exactly. What do you mean, Chan—assassinated?"

"Assassinated," Chan Benson said, and he no longer looked quite so benevolent, nor quite so gentle. The change was slow, and it was still going on; his voice became harder as he spoke. "Killed. Dead. Assassinated. It means what it says, Pollorine, and it doesn't say anything more."

He looked over at me. I held out my hand and, almost absently, he put the paper into it.

I was hired: the job was started.

I looked down. It was a piece of newstape stuff, that thick shiny material the newswire computers print on. It said what Chan Benson had said.

I was filing names as I went along: Benson, Pollorine, Timmins—the tall man—and Betty, which was all the name I had for the horse-faced woman. It was Betty who spoke first.

"Well, Knave?" she said. She'd dropped the Mister. They did, mostly, when the shooting started; Hell, I did myself. "What do you advise now?" It was a remarkably nasty tone, considering I'd barely met the woman.

Benson began to say something, but I got in ahead of him.

"I advise getting the Hell to the Embassy offices," I said, "and filling me in. By closed car, if possible—what do you have here, wheels or ground-effects stuff?"

It turned out to be wheels, and I shouldn't have had to ask the question: ground-effects winds are not wanted where you have a lot of snakes for pedestrians.

Wheeled cars aren't much wanted, either. It isn't the pollution problem—as usual with wheelies, Haven IV was on electrics—it's the native problem. You can swerve to avoid hitting a human being who's blundered out into the center of the road.

You can swerve to avoid a snake, too—if you can see him.

The speed limit on Haven IV was a posted, enforced fifteen miles per hour. It was like the old saying: Violators Will Be Disposed Of. Traffic offenses did not draw fines and lectures on Haven IV. Some of them drew instant death penalties.

We moseyed along to the Embassy, all four of us packed into the rear because we had an official chauffeur—a disapproving sort of man, whose name I never did get. On the way, I got filled in on the Crown Jewels, to some extent.

The trouble was that the process kept getting interrupted. Every few seconds either Pollorine or Gorgial (which turned out to be Betty's other handle) would break into Chan Benson's lucid explanations with something like:

"Good Lord, Chan—if Tal's gone, who's going to be next?"

Or (from Betty Gorgial): "Chan, what do you think it means? Now that—this—has happened, I mean: what does it mean?"

It was a question I wanted to try answering; but in order to do that I had to amass some facts. Benson pointed that out, calmly, and got nothing much for his work; she and the bowler hat kept popping off all the way into the city, all the way to the Embassy garage.

That's right: garage. It was my second bit of advice: "Don't stop in front and go in through the front door. Is there a closed garage and an entrance to the building from there?"

It turned out—no surprise; there usually is—that there was, and my advice was taken with only the slightest mutter from Pollorine about the loss of dignity.

"Apparently this news has put you people into some sort of danger," I said. "When I know a little more I'll be able, maybe, to assess the danger, and maybe even do something about it. For now, put your dignity in storage; whoever's just potted General Tal will find it a good deal harder to get at you from inside a garage."

Actually, of course, a determined assassin could have potted all four of us at any point between the Embarcation Building and the Embassy garage—it was a closed car, but it had windows that didn't seem to be bullet-proof, and fifteen miles an hour makes it very easy for a man standing on a street-corner with a beamer or a powerful slug gun and a fairly good eye. My move would have been to pot the chauffeur first, and get the rest of us as we scrambled.

I didn't point any of that out.

And we reached the garage safely.

The Embassy—not quite.

The chauffeur swung the car into the garage— the self-opening doors going shut behind us— and over to a recharge post at the far end. As usual, he turned the car round and backed in so that the rear fender just nudged the recharge post as the car stopped.

And the damn thing exploded.

It wasn't an accident: there is no way in the world for an electric-auto recharge post to explode in the course of nature.

Somebody had booby-trapped the thing—it went on contact, like a land mine.

And it sprayed bits of itself all over the garage. Shrapnel: the thing was mostly steel construction.

Most of the pieces fell on other cars, landed in the walls, bounced off the metal of our car—expended harmlessly.

One piece—long, thin and sharp—came straight through the rear window and into the back of Pollorine's head.

He was dead before he could make a sound.

CHAPTER TWO

And everybody began to do the obvious things, none of which made much sense. There was quite a lot of screaming and shouting from Betty Gorgial and the chauffeur, and some even from Chan Benson, whose generally quiet carriage had begun to win me over by contrast to just about everything else. There was also a mad scramble to be first out of the damned car. Pollorine, tilted forward a little rather than slumped—maybe he wore a girdle: I never found out, and don't much want to, really—provided the rest of us with a sterling example of sense, but I was the only one following the example. And even I had to get a little noisy.

It took, for instance, several screams of "Stop!" in a variety of tones, directed at one or another of the living personnel, before some of the shoving wore out. I had to grab Betty Gorgial's shoulder and haul her back inside one-handed; but at last we were all safely back in the car, chauffeur in the front seat with Gorgial for company, Chan Benson sitting at the right in back, Pollorine at the left, still dead, and Gerald Knave, about three-fifths deaf, smack in the middle as usual.

A little more time went by before everybody ran out of vocal chords—Betty Gorgial didn't run down last, by the way: the chauffeur did, rattling on in a wildly high-pitched voice like an English horn in heat—and there we were: peace, blessed peace, with loved ones far away, as the old tombstone says. I swallowed once or twice to correct a slight tendency toward rasp, since I'd hauled everybody but Betty Gorgial into the car again by voice, which is more of a strain than doing it by hand.

"All right," I said to my captive audience. "We are now, for the moment, safe."

"Safe!" Gorgial shrieked, twisting round in her seat to aim the speech at me: we were almost as far apart as you can get in that model car, but it wasn't far enough. "With Ernest dead? A corpse—all of us huddled inside a car with a corpse—and he calls it safe!"

Chan Benson cleared his throat. He looked, still the sadly benevolent uncle, at Pollorine's leaning figure. "I take it there's no doubt that he is—that it really is a corpse?" he said.

"No doubt at all," I told him. Pulse zero, respiration zero, I'd rolled up the eyelids—one, anyhow—and seen blank white; and from the position and angle of the splinter still sticking out of the back of his skull, I hadn't really needed to make any tests at all. It's not a jab you recover from, not ever, if it goes deep enough— and that doesn't have to be very damned deep. "Ernest Pollorine. Can somebody tell me a little about him? Just who he worked for, what position he held—that sort of thing, for openers?"

The Gorgial voice hadn't climbed down from its volume peak. "The man's insane!" she shouted. "Questions—sitting here—at a time like this! Pollorine—General Tal—" She waved both arms in the air, brushing the car roof. "Knave, why don't you do something?"

"I am doing something," I said. "I've got you, and Mr. Benson, and our chauffeur, nicely collected in the only safe place I know about, and I'm trying to find out something that will give me an odds-on guess about safety somewhere else. We can't stay here forever; sooner or later, somebody would come looking."

"Safe place!" The same voice, the same shriek. "This car—with a dead man—"

Dead men are usually very dependable people to be around. They will not rise up and bash you over the head, and they will not scream the sillies into your ears. "I know this car is safe," I said, maybe not quite as mildly as Chan Benson would have managed it, "because the recharge post exploded." Before Betty Gorgial could wind herself up for some more objections, I went on: "Somebody booby-trapped the thing. It's shot its bolt. And nobody'd bother to do that—a tricky job right inside the Embassy garage—if he'd booby-trapped the car instead. The car's safe: the recharge post can't explode twice, because it isn't there now, and anybody in the garage who wants to pot one or more of us will have a harder job if we're inside a darkened car —" of course the interior lighting, such as it was, had been wiped out by the explosion—"than if we're trying to find some other hiding-place in a very bare garage." The place had two other cars at (intact) recharge posts, three or four posts awaiting more little electrics, and a couple of columns: imitation concrete, at a fast guess.

And, away over to the right, far back along the wall, a flight of four steps leading to a door with a small lighting unit over it. By no very special set of deductions, the entrance to the Embassy; but I didn't want any of our little crowd standing at that door, open or shut, nicely targeted by the little overhead light, until—at least—some time had passed. Most gunmen are reasonably nervous types: there was a fair limit to the amount of time I could expect one to spend sitting and waiting to fire.

And any small facts I collected while waiting were just so much gravy. The right facts might even give me enough material to take a flying guess at what was waiting for our little party on the other side of that door.

It wasn't sensible to expect Betty Gorgial to take that in, all or any significant part, but I laid most of it out anyhow. Chan Benson seemed to be following me, and the chauffeur was the type who calmed down when surrounded by any reasonably sane-sounding voice saying things slowly and blandly enough.

But I laid it out in pieces. Gorgial erupted every now and again, and the chauffeur had an attack or two of the gibbers; I was glad of a few of the interruptions, because they were Chan Benson's, and they were informative.

Twenty minutes after the explosion, we were still in the car. I had a little file of data on Ernest

Pollorine (First Undersecretary for Extrahuman Affairs, Embassy staff: career diplomat, assigned to Haven IV six years ago, after a tour of duty as Comity Relations Undersecretary on Apelles—a fully-human world, and one he must have hated to leave—unmarried, no pets, no known close friends, a small-time chess hobbyist and a slightly larger-time gourmet, or gourmand, take your pick) from Benson, an even smaller file on working Embassy personnel—the people on the other side of the door, and the entire list of most-likely-suspects for planting a bomb in an Embassy-garage recharge post—and what felt like a rather large library of shrieks, complaints, impassioned pleas, insults, howls and just plain whimpers. The library had been contributed by Betty Gorgial and the chauffeur —in memoriam, I suppose, Ernest Pollorine, and I don't think he'd have approved. Not really his style, as far as I'd had a chance to judge it.

I wasn't going to get much more; the slightly cramped quarters, the enforced inactivity, and the corpse—probably in reverse order—were shredding even the Benson nerves.

So I spun things out for five more minutes, by my watch. Any time limit you set on an assassin's patience is your own invention, if only because you haven't met the man; but twenty-five minutes felt fairly safe. And, as I'd said, sooner or later somebody was going to come looking.

The explosion had drawn no crowd: the garage was normally a noisy spot; even electrics being less than totally silent, a herd of them all in one place can stir up a racket. So the place was fairly well soundproofed.

One small advantage: except by sight—seeing our car head for the garage and go in—nobody knew for sure we'd arrived.

The twenty-five-minute mark came. I said: "Everybody out—very slowly, and very quietly," and jostled my car door open with a minimum of noisy fuss. I think Chan Benson had a minute of wanting to take Pollorine along with us, but he talked himself out of it with no help from me. Betty Gorgial was the only really noisy member of the crew; she stamped and rustled and slammed things, and something she wore—a bangle or a medal, I couldn't tell because she was behind me—kept going *clink* all the way, except for the times when it went *clonk*. We stayed fairly well bunched up (my instructions: strung out in a file, we were that much easier to pop off), hit the four stairs, and went on from there with a minimum of laziness. Chan Benson reached out to open the door, and I said: "Allow me," and did the job instead, and went in following my own arm, very low and slanting left. The others followed: Benson, the damned fool, had stood under that light and handed in Gorgial and the chauffeur before crossing over and—very nicely, too—shutting the door with barely a sound.

I heard him lock it: not a silent operation unless you are very, very good and highly trained.

Then—none of us having been shot at, exploded, or even the teeniest bit annoyed—I took the Hell of a deep breath, and looked around.

Headquarters?

CHAPTER THREE

The place looked, at first glance, fully human: about like any Embassy, anywhere. We'd come into a side corridor, less than six feet long, and traveled along it until it led us to a large open space. Again, I went in first, fast and low, and again nobody was shooting at us. This sort of thing can look very silly when it is not followed by explosions or beams of one sort or another; but I have less objection to looking silly than I have to not staying alive.

Standing in a small clump at one side of what turned out to be the Reception Hall (high ceiling, marble-type walls dotted with sconces, a central desk, any number of couches scattered around the walls, and a luxurious pile rug, plain royal blue), we were barely noticed, for the first second or two.

Then the man sitting at the desk did a small take, and greeted all of us in general (some sort of invisible mike at the desk, I supposed). We went to meet him.

Chan Benson said we wanted Reception Area B, and we were not to be disturbed, and the man at the desk—young, looking bored, wearing a bright yellow suit that didn't do nearly as much for him as he thought it did, and my guess is that he had his hair waved once a month—said "Certainly, certainly," and I had to step in and tell him we didn't want that at all.

His eyebrows went up, rather slowly and elegantly, and he turned to Benson. "Gerald Knave," Benson said. "Please accede to his requirements." I can't remember having heard it phrased so elegantly.

I told the receptionist that the first thing we wanted was a pass for *me* to get into Reception Area B, and check it the Hell out; after that, we could all meet again. I was bothered by having to leave my charges in that empty big room, but I did tell them, as I was going off, to stay together, and stay against a wall near the garage.

"But, Knave," Betty Gorgial said. "Isn't this just silly? I mean, after all—"

"I don't take any chances I don't have to," I said. "While I'm running this show, neither do you. Nine times out of ten, it doesn't matter what you do: the tenth time, you die." I gave her a very polite smile—why make enemies?—and she shut up.

By then I had my pass, or at least permission from the receptionist, who was going to phone ahead. (I didn't mind that: just then, I didn't have enough information to tell him not to. Hell, if somebody did shoot at me en route, it'd give me something to work with in the way of facts. If I lived, of course, but that's what I was being paid so nicely for. The chances I take are the ones I damn well have to.) I went off to my left, through an arch and double doors and around a corner, and after a while—during which I was not shot at, and passed nobody except a cheerful-looking, ugly girl carrying a sheaf of papers and what looked like a small, light rug draped over a surreal metal framework, long and thin and very weird indeed—I came to a set of imitation-wood doors, opened them, found myself in an airlock sort of space between those doors and an equally large set of glassex ones, opened the glassex jobs, and spent about half an hour checking out Reception Area B, chairs, sofas, desks, odd plants, light fixtures, and three of those surreal metal-and-rug arrangements, as well as a telephone, six or seven reference books and a few tapes. . . .

You get the idea. All perfectly safe. I went back to the phone and picked it up. After no more than four or five days' worth of confusion I managed to reach the receptionist, and told him to give everybody else the go-ahead—and to instruct them, as from me, to take exactly the route he'd laid out for me, no short cuts, no sudden changes of plan.

He said "Certainly, certainly," and I think he was about to hang up.

My end of the phone made a sound like a dull *crump*, followed by a crackle of static, and then nothing at all: not a disconnect, but that airless space-between-the-galaxies effect you get when the whole line is dead.

I didn't waste any time.

They hadn't moved, as far as I could tell, when I hit the Reception Hall again, at a dead run. They were huddled together against a wall, and they didn't even seem to be breathing very much.

But the receptionist had moved.

The receptionist was all the Hell over the room, in damn small pieces. His desk was just barely recognizable as the remains of a desk. About where his chair would have been, a small fire was burning merrily.

"All right," I said. "Now come with me."

That took some more effort. Everybody wanted to stay around and watch the fire, and notify somebody, and wring his or her hands, and so forth. When it was finally borne in on them that the only way to notify anybody was to come with me, and maybe find a working phone —if the desk explosion hadn't knocked out the whole network—they began to come around, and shortly we were on our way.

The explosion hadn't knocked out the phone network, though there were a lot of holes in it, temporarily. Most of the real circuitry and little boxes sat in the basement, apparently still safe. I could pick up the Reception Area B phone and find it working again, and hand it to Chan Benson for notifications.

After he'd directed a small crew to take care of things, as far as possible, I went and sat down on a comfortable chair and tried to look relaxed, and motioned the others to collapse as well. I got no resistance from Betty Gorgial, or from the chauffeur: after that single flare-up back in the big hall, they were both walking around stunned. A little too much had been happening, a little too fast.

Either Chan Benson didn't stun easily, or he was the brains behind everything, if it took brains. (If it didn't, he might have been, if you see what I mean: but if anything that had happened was following any sort of sensible direction, it wasn't his; or he wouldn't have been in the car. Nobody could have loaded that post to pick off Ernest Pollorine: accidents don't care who they happen to.) At any rate, he sat down, and took a few deep breaths, and refused my offer of a cigarette, and began to answer questions. I had about five hundred questions.

Most of the answers you've already had: I wanted to know about the Tocks, about the theft I'd been called in for, and suchlike background. I ended up wanting to know a good deal more about the Tocks, but I told myself I could check out a library, preferably non-exploding, or a couple of tame experts, a little later on. Or, maybe, I could just ask the Tocks themselves: they didn't sound as if they'd mind.

I also wanted to know about the receptionist —in more detail than I'd had in that brief rundown on Embassy personnel away back in our nice, safe car—and about General Tal. The receptionist seemed to be no more than a receptionist, with a taste for diplomatic surroundings: he'd been with the Embassy for three years, his first off-world job (he'd been born on Sanderson, away back near the Home Worlds and the center of the Comity). General Tal, as you might expect, was something else again.

Haven IV didn't have much of a military establishment. The Tocks didn't need one—and in

any case would have come up with their own.
But wherever human beings go, one way or another, a few professionals follow—lawyers, policemen, and an army. On worlds with a higher
water-to-land ratio than Earth, a navy.

We're not Tocks. We have lawbreakers by the
carload lot, and we also have this nagging feeling
that we are going to be fighting somebody or
other reasonably soon.

This nagging feeling is usually correct: there
have been periods called Peace here and there in
human history, but what Peace usually means is
that the fighting is happening somewhere else
just now. It'll get to wherever you are shortly; if
you are very, very lucky, it may then move on,
leaving you (slightly battered) back in Peace.

Wherever there are human-alien relations to
consider, the nagging feeling cranks itself up to a
nice, shrill whine. Once in a while there is a fight
between human beings and whatever alien race
has happened along, and sometimes the fight
gets big enough to be called a war. Not very
often—but it only takes once. After that, the professional fighting men go wherever we've met an
alien race, and wait around, just in case.

Half the time, they're a barely tolerated
group. The natives are friendly, the colonists are
busy colonizing, and these crude people fenced
off into a set of barracks are no better than
pugnacious brutes.

The other half of the time, they lead the pro-
cession. This happens when the natives are distinctly not friendly; it also happens when some
of the colonists begin to feel less than friendly

toward other colonists. And it happens, very rarely, when the military establishment is being run by someone like Horgai Tal.

Most generals—like most top-rated men in any craft—are intelligent people. Most of them are also pugnacious, self-centered, and given to treating civilians exactly as if they were untrained enlisted personnel—a technical term that translates to Brainless and Useless.

A very few of them, in any age, are different. Ever since Cincinnatus resigned and went back to the farm, there have been generals who fought when they had to—and damned well, as a rule—and tried their very best to avoid fighting all the rest of the time. Empathy is a dangerous quality for a military man: if you have to commit troops, it's a good deal less strain if you can avoid thinking of them as individual human beings. But if you can manage it, and stay sane, you might just turn into one of those special wonders: Cincinnatus, Pompey, Washington, Kutuzov, Marshall (George, or S. L. A., take your pick)—or General Horgai Tal.

Tal was a good deal more than the head of Haven IV's small military force (recruited from Haven II, which meant they were tied in with the Embassy, not the Consulate; it took me a while to keep the difference straight in my head, and a longer while to find out what sort of difference it made). Tal was, for all intents and purposes, head of the whole Haven IV human settlement. People who agreed on nothing else agreed on General Tal: people who had no respect for each other found themselves united in respect for this one man.

It wasn't unanimous—very little is, and that little tends not to be voluntary: the desire for oxygen, for instance—but it came about as close as such things ever do. Tal's place as ranking General of the local army could be filled easily enough, almost automatically; but Tal's place as head of the settlement on Haven IV might not be the sort of place you could find any other human being to fill.

Ernest Pollorine was, in terms of that society, a replaceable piece; the dead receptionist was even more replaceable. Horgai Tal came as close as I could imagine to being irreplaceable, in that society at that time.

For some reason, that small set of facts stuck in my head like a rotten tune: I kept replaying the thing without wanting to. It had a large red label on it, reading Important.

I had no idea why.

But by the time I'd had this rundown I was dealing with a large and frantic situation. The explosion of that front desk had been heard all over the Embassy, more or less; it took a little time for people to get down to the Reception area from everywhere else in the damned building, but once they did it was no time at all before some helpful type filled them in on current events, and Gerald Knave was the leading current event. Reception Area B was crowded in five minutes, and in five more it was doing a decorous imitation of a howling mob—decorous, I suppose, because diplomatic personnel get the habit of acting diplomatically whether or not it makes sense at the time.

For a short while, I was busy fending off the world, explaining to anybody and everybody that an explosion had happened, which was both what they knew and what I wanted to find out about. I didn't tell them anything else because I didn't have anything else worth telling—except for the first explosion, back in the garage, and anybody who didn't know about that one yet would be just a shade more peaceful, and more manageable.

Betty Gorgial, crowded off into a corner, was doing a brisk trade of her own in What and Where and When among people who hadn't got to Gerald Knave yet, or hadn't spotted him, or wanted to talk to somebody familiar (though Gorgial was a member of the Consulate, not the Embassy: the settlement on Haven IV was just small enough so that most people knew most of the others, at least by sight); and Gorgial had no such reluctance: she was, very clearly, filling everybody in on everything, all the way back from the receptionist to Ernest Pollorine to (for anybody who hadn't got the news as it came in) General Tal, and for all I knew straight on back to Cain and Abel. She was the center of a slowly growing knot of thoroughly panicked human beings, making more noise than you might believe and losing their decorum bit by bit.

Chan Benson, lost someplace in the mob, seemed to be doing his best to calm people down, but his best was just too calm to have any noticeable effect; I spotted him for a few seconds at a time, but I couldn't hear him, and I doubt that the person he was talking to could do much better. The third time I saw him I signalled to him; the fifth time, he caught it, nodded and started edging toward the entrance arch, against the incoming flow.

It struck me that the crowd would have to level off after a while: after all, how many people were there in the Embassy? But the place looked as if Ripley's Marching Chinese were packing into it, and no end in sight; when I met Benson at the arch I was ripe for escape.

The question was: where to? I had a tiny file of facts on Embassy personnel, and I was going to have to get a matching set on Consulate personnel (but, please God, not from Betty Gorgial), and on the military establishment, the police, the grocer, the butcher, the baker, the tailor, the fifteen or twenty auto-repair shops (all doing a thriving business, all the time: a car in less than perfect shape was an ambulant criminal offense, minimum penalty five years in the local penitentiary, not noted for lavish displays of gracious living), and, endlessly, so forth.

I was, tentatively, willing to take the word of everybody who had ever seen a Tock that I didn't need a dossier on the natives. Tentatively because I dislike taking anybody's word but my own that any given assemblage of molecules in the universe is not dangerous. But it looked as if "tentative" was going to have to do: everything, so far, had happened to human beings, in human areas of habitation—ignoring the theft of the Crown Jewels, which seemed to have started everything, but didn't seem to be connected to anything, either. I wasn't much worried about the possibility of being stolen, and one theft was all that had happened among the Tocks.

Clearly enough—at least until I could begin to get a few things straightened out—I had no business setting up headquarters anywhere except among the Tocks—if they'd have me, and if their living habits were such that I could manage to adapt for a while.

That much was clear by the time I hit the entrance arch. What was also clear, as I headed Chan Benson off to the left, along what looked to be the least-travelled route—still going against the tide, by God—was the immediate problem:

How in Hell do I get there?

CHAPTER FOUR

My God, somebody shot at me on the way.

I didn't really expect that. I took precautions against it, because if it is even remotely possible and if I can think of it I will take precautions against it—which may be half of the secret of doing well enough at my trade not to get killed—but the precautions had been no more than gestures. A car had exploded, a desk had exploded, a General had been assassinated, and, (to start things off at the beginning of all this madness) a job lot of Crown non-Jewels had been stolen. But this had nothing to do with me, except as it affected my bank balances. I'd been hired. To find the non-Jewels, and to smoothe things over between humanity and the Tocks.

All very simple. I suppose you could cover it under one or another heading of my business card: *Survivor*, I mean. I was making it possible for the human colony on Haven IV to survive, maybe. Or I was making sure that Tock-human relations survived. I'm not picky; if it sounds interesting (and sometimes if it doesn't), and if it pays the bills, I will cheerfully turn up.

And I will cheerfully wait for Betty Gorgial to get the Consulate on the colony 3V phone. The

Embassy, where I was and where most of the Tock-human relations were centered, had "protected" cars about as good as the one I'd already ridden in. This was not good enough.

The Consulate—because the Consulate thought like that—had truly protected cars. Bulletproof, beamproof, reflective . . . well, if you hit one of them with a small atomic explosion it might get dented, but nobody was willing to bet on it. All in all, a very nice, enclosed little womb for Gerald Knave (when I thought about it I felt a little like one of the fish in the Crown non-Jewels, but I don't light up that way, and the car's ecology wasn't really balanced over the long haul, like two days), and I had only one little instruction.

"The driver is to enter the garage," I said. "Nowhere else. He is to charge up at the Consulate, and not recharge anywhere until he has reached the Tock settlement and dropped me off and gone away." I mean, why take chances with any more surprises, like exploding recharge posts? The car could take it (everyone assured me, Betty Gorgial most vocally), but—well, why give it a chance to have to?

Gorgial nodded very seriously and in a totally businesslike fashion. Being given orders in an ongoing situation was something she understood very well. It kept her quiet, for one thing; I filed that one away for future use, being fairly sure I was going to need it.

Then she got on the phone again, and relayed my "demands," which is what she called them—I'd have preferred "instructions," or even "requests," but why be picky?—and told me everything was in good shape, and that the car would arrive in ten minutes. "Possibly eight," she said, and I thanked her gravely.

It was more like half an hour.

Seems the first car sent out started up its motor and nudged its recharge post, to spur it on for the task ahead—and the post blew up. The driver wasn't hurt, but he was (Gorgial told me) a little shaken up, and the car, while quite unhurt, would have to have a full going-over by mechanics.

"Wonderful," I said. It was the first repeat: two recharge explosions. I filed the fact, for whatever good it might do me. "Did anything else happen?"

Gorgial shrugged. "Nothing," she said. "Another car is ready, and another driver. Nothing else at all—unless you count the garage mechanic."

"What about the garage mechanic?" I said.

"He was in the garage," she said. The conversation was beginning to sound like a late nineteenth century routine called But The Dog Died.

"He was in the garage," I said. "Fine. What did he see?"

She shrugged again. "We have no idea," she said. "He was blown to bits by the explosion." Her voice was perfectly calm. "But, as I say, nothing else of any importance happened."

I had not been fond of Betty Gorgial. Every passing minute, it seemed, gave me another reason for my attitude.

But in half an hour or so, a car nosed its way into the garage, carefully avoiding the recharge posts, and I opened the Embassy-garage door and came down four steps and walked over and got in.

Alone. Chan Benson had suggested that he might be useful as an interpreter (though the Tocks, it seemed, spoke English of a sort) and general explainer, and Betty Gorgial was very insistent indeed; I heard a good deal about her duty as Consulate representative to serve as mediator between a stranger and this group of alien beings. . . .

And, as they say, so forth.

I said the same thing several times. "I'm going to have to get to know them," I told enquirers. "And that means going in alone. It means developing a relationship between me and the Tocks, one we'll have to find for ourselves."

I haven't said "developing a relationship" since I can remember, and don't want to ever again; but it sounded like admissible jargon, and made for a smooth explanation. I sounded properly regretful (truly, to Chan Benson; lying my overworked head off, to Gorgial), and after a time I got my way.

The reason I didn't want to give anyone was obvious enough. The Tocks—non-violent, non-tricky, as far as I could find out—were not causing all this Hell. Human beings were, somehow and for some idiotic reason I would figure out when I had time.

And I didn't know, for sure, which human beings. So I didn't want any of them along with me.

So I went across the garage all alone (and nobody shot at me; it was now a fair certainty that
either a) there was no assassin lurking in that
place, or b) he suffered from Sleeping Sickness),
climbed into a car that looked a little like an ancient Mercedes and a little like a small tank, and
greeted the driver with: "Okay. Let's go."

He said: "Yes, Sir." The Consulate, I
thought, was half a military outpost by itself:
this young man was sitting straight up, eyes
ahead, hands in approved position on the wheel,
and a snap in his voice you didn't expect in civilian life.

All right: I filed that, too. The driver did a few
things and the car started. We weren't using its
brain even for the automatic stretch of highway
—we'd used the other car's, of course. "Manual," I said. "Manual all the way. So I can
watch what happens."

He never blinked. "Yes, Sir," he said. He was
a stocky, short man with black hair and rather
small eyes. I didn't think I was going to warm to
him, but I didn't think I would ever have to. The
car started, and swung out of the garage, and
there we were on the street.

Two blocks away, a beam lit up the right rear
window, next to where I was sitting.

No damage. The driver just kept going.

"Hey," I said.

"Do you wish to report the incident?" he
asked me. Sounded as if he got shot at every day,
twice on Sundays. "The 3V linkage available
just before you—"

There was a phone and suchlike sunk into the

upholstery before me, the rear of the front seat.

I phoned the Embassy (I think the driver disapproved: the back of his neck said loudly that I should have tapped the Consulate instead) and reported. I advised them not to go out hunting for whoever'd tried to do me in. "He'll be long gone; and if you wander around out there you may be a target for somebody else."

"He?" Gorgial said.

Some of my best friends have even nuttier religions than FemLib. Not that Gorgial was going to be one of my best friends, but . . . "All right," I said. "He or she."

"Thank you," she said, offensively. It's easy to say offensively: try it. It will make enemies for you, but go ahead and try it. Be the first kid on your block to be done in by an enraged group of your peers.

"Welcome." End conversation. I looked around: not much of a view, mostly low hedges and bare streets, now and then a snake about three feet long, less often a human being, walking from here to there. I began to file the snakes: every bit of information, even on appearance, might help when we hit our destination.

I was going to meet the King.

CHAPTER FIVE

"This Tock settlement—" I began, partway there.

"They don't call it a settlement," the driver said.

"Camp, then," I said. "Gathering place. Group."

"None of those," he said.

I did my own small shrug. "All right, then, what do they call it?"

"A city," he said.

Quite properly put down, and I felt it. The city's name was not pronounceable, but the Tocks had worked out a name we could use. It was called London.

Wonderful. London: where the King lives. Right?

The city of London, on Haven IV, inhabited by several thousand three-foot-long snakes, or almost-snakes. The city of London, from which the Crown non-Jewels had been stolen.

I began to wonder about seeing the Tower. Or at least a Beefeater.

Well, it passed the time. Kept me up with my ancient history, too.

*   *   *

Nassanank, King of the Tocks (except for every nine days, as, more or less, explained previously): a dark, nearly black snake, with a very shiny carapace, and a length a bit over three feet. I think he had fifty or sixty feet, but it was hard to tell; we were sitting around the King's Private Apartments, having a chat, and Nassanank was fully buttoned up. (I discovered what that odd, long shape with a rug on it—the one I'd seen someone carrying back at the Embassy—was for. It was a Tock chair. Or couch. Or, for all I really knew, loveseat. Take your choice.)

Nassanank was coiled on his—throne, I guess, since it was gold and glittery and had a silver-and-glitter thick-pile rug, talking things over with me quite calmly.

"But I don't see, Mr. Knave," he was saying, "what I ought to do—or what I have any slightest duty to do—about these deaths in the human colony. Except, of course, deplore them —which I do officially, and here state that I do personally as well." He shifted into a more tightened coil: anger, apparently, or disgust. I hadn't got too good at reading Tock expressions, not then. "Killing!" he said, in the voice you or I might use to say *child molesting.* "It is a terrible thing."

"It's worse than that," I said. I was sitting in a chair constructed for humans, and padded with as many cushions as your average massage parlor resting-bed. No: more. And better, too. The Tocks did proud by their visitors—even the visitors, like me, with bad news.

"Worse?" Nassanank said, with a pretty fair hiss.

"It isn't only killing," I said. "It's connected with the theft of your Crown Jewels, Sire."

"Theft?" the snake said. "And—please, you needn't call me Sire. My name's Nassanank."

"And I'm Knave. Or Jerry, as you like. Most people say Knave."

He nodded. It's a very odd sight, a snake nodding: more like an undulation. But we'd been talking for a bit, and I thought I could get used to it.

"Knave, then," he said. Good pronunciation. I couldn't have done as well with Tock talk, from all I'd been able to find out. I lit one more of my lovely red cigarettes (Inoson Smoking Pleasure Tubes, Guaranteed Harmless, and, in any case, dyed red. Cigarettes, if you don't mind), ignoring the fancy, gem-studded narghile Nassanank had provided me with when he found out, almost at once, that I was a smoker. I can't smoke through a narghile without being on the ground, with my legs crossed, and seldom want to. My lovely cigarettes would do.

At any rate, they were expensive enough for the Kingly Presence.

"And it's more than killing, Nassanank," I said. I was beginning to like this snake—well, this Tock. I hadn't met Queen Jessiss yet, but I had hopes. "It's the connection with the theft. If that hadn't happened, the killings wouldn't have started: they came one after the other, and I don't really want to believe in that sort of coincidence."

"What theft?" he said, looking straight at me.

I blinked. Then I got it. "Theft," I said. "It's a word meaning 'robbery,' or 'stealing.' I meant the Crown Jewels—the ones that are missing."

He nodded again. "And you are sure that a theft—" he used the word carefully, fitting it into his vocabulary— "is the cause of the disappearance?" he asked me.

I sighed, just a little. "What else?"

"Inadvertence, perhaps," Nassananak said. "Or the operation of some natural law of which we know nothing, a law which caused the—what you have called the Crown Jewels—to disappear."

Madness. But sanity has never been a test of my friends; and the lack of it wasn't going to interfere with the job I was on, either. I needed the pay—if only to buy more Inoson Smoking Pleasure Tubes, Guaranteed Harmless.

"Let's leave the matter for later discussion," I said, after a second or so. Madness is digestible only slowly. "But the Jewels and these killings are connected."

Nassanak nodded again—no, this time it was just a squirm, to get more comfortable on the silver deep-pile. "They may be," he said. "But do you think that the Jewels, as you say, in human hands would force the humans to kill each other? We have never postulated such an effect."

Another blink, another second's pause. "No, Sire—Nassanank," I said. "I have no idea what the connection is, but I doubt that it's anything as simple as cause-and-effect: the Jewels loose cause human killings. It's another sort of structure."

"Well," Nassanank sighed with a slight background hiss, "you know your species better than I can. And—if there is a connection—then I would be glad to be of aid to you, if I can. It is true that returning the—ah—Jewels must be a human affair; but putting an end to this *killing*—" same emphasis— "is equally important to me, and I am sure to Jessiss and to our valued Medium. And, I do not doubt, to the new King-and-Queen, in a few days."

I'd been filled in on the lottery, or whatever it was. "It's due in a few days?" I said, with some apprehension. God alone knew what would bust loose during that one day of fairly random rule.

"Three, to be exact," Nassanank said, quite calmly. "Does the time make a difference to you or to your work?"

I thought about it. "Well," I said, very cautiously—never tread on native toes if you can avoid it, whether they have toes or not— "it might. I can't say for certain."

"Ah," Nassanank said, squirming and nodding all at once. He even unflapped and wiggled a few legs, just for relaxation. "Then we shall proclaim it for two days, instead."

He must have read my face. Two days was no better than three; in fact, it was a good deal worse. What I needed was time. And he saw that I hadn't liked his well-meant suggestion. (Well-meant? Unique: the Tocks had never offered to shift the lottery date for anyone before, for any reason—nor hinted that it could be shifted.)

"This is not satisfactory?" he said.

He sounded as if he really felt sorry about it. Well, so did I. "What I need is time," I told him. "As much time as possible—before the—the lottery."

"A human need?" the Tock King said.

I sighed again. "You might call it that," I said. Talking to aliens—especially, I was beginning to see, Tocks—was the verbal equivalent of a funhouse mirror.

"Then I am filled with sorrow," he told me. "I can give you no more time. I can give you less, a little—by one day, or at most a day and a quarter. But not more."

I was still a little shaken up. Not by the explosions and such—in my checkered career, or whatever it is, I have met a lot of explosions, and you get sort of used to them.

By the Tock city. I haven't told you about that. I will; wait around.

So, shaken up, I said a stupid thing. I said: "Why?"

Ever seen a snake shrug with casual helplessness? Even odder than seeing him nod.

"It is quite clear," he said. "Postponement would add to the uncertainty of our society; we Tocks would be disturbed by that new uncertainty."

"And wouldn't pushing the time forward do the same thing?" I said. "After all, it's the same sort of change, either way—isn't it?"

"I see," Nassanank said. "You do not understand. But—it is not the same thing, not at all. Take an equivalent case: take the King's Gift."

"The fish that make up the Crown Jewels."

"Exactly," he said. I was a good pupil. "A Tock who finds such a Gift presents it to the King, in effect, and thereby gains some little time of additional work before he must retire. If, instead, he lost work-time—if he had to retire sooner—would this be an equivalent?"

"Well," I said, "no. But—"

"Time, Knave," he said, "is unidirectional. Like radiation."

That one was going to take more time than I had. In my experience, radiation was not unidirectional. Unless the Tocks meant something else by the word (improbable) or knew something about radiation in general that the human race didn't know (quite probable indeed, and frightening as Hell). "But—" I began, fishing for some more information, if I could understand it enough to bring it back.

"Time is unidirectional, surely," Nassanank said. "We age—as I understand human beings think of the process. We do not un-age, so to speak."

A line from a parody of a famous preSpace poet drifted idly, and insanely, into my head.

As we get older, we do not get any younger.

True. Irrelevant, I hoped to Hell, but true. "But—what do you mean, 'as human beings think of the process'?"

One more shrug: a casual, complex ripple on the deep pile. "We think of it differently," he said. "As maturity. Only the unfortunate among us, the few unfortunate, age. For the most part, we mature: we grow in some ways younger, in some ways older. But it is a unidirectional process: maturity is subject, like all else, to time's arrow."

"In some ways younger?" I said.

"Of course," he said. "Whichever ways one chooses. For myself, I have chosen to grow younger in physical terms, in terms of certain emotions, and in relation to the Medium I share with my Queen. Jessiss, on the other hand—but such decisions are private matters. I would not injure her privacy."

"I wouldn't dream of it, myself," I said. I hoped that I hadn't understood him. Choosing to grow physically younger . . . choosing to grow younger 'in relation to' something else. . . .

It sounded just a little as if the Tocks had a hammerlock on the rules of the universe, as understood F. O. B. humanity's Home Worlds. But —they couldn't be all that powerful, could they?

If they were, what had anybody needed me for?

And when that question occurred to me, another one up and bit me on the nose at once:

Just what did they think I was?

The question didn't last long (answer: because a race is ahead of humanity in some things, it need not be ahead of humanity, or even up to it, in others); but, while it lasted, I had myself a fine, thorough case of the shivers.

A case, I might add, not caused by the damned climate of Haven IV. A Hell of a place to stay.

Well . . . the sooner I wrapped everything up . . .

Whatever (my mind reminded me) 'every-thing' was. . . .

CHAPTER SIX

And before anybody does anything else, stop and take a look at a Tock city. It won't make all the sense you think it ought to, but you're in good company: nobody understands Tocks except Tocks. The place was absolutely dazzling, as far as I was concerned, and made no sort of sense, not when you got below the surface and began to dig for particulars.

And now and then the surface wasn't so very damned sensible, either.

Look: the streets and the buildings are interconnected. This is not easy to picture, but if you've ever seen a long traffic underpass of a tunnel going North-South under a surface road going East-West—it was a little like that. You'd walk along the street for a while, noticing that intersections seemed a bit weird now and again, and then you wouldn't be in the street any more: you'd be walking through a tunnel (and very stooped over: Tock streets are easily as wide as good human boulevards, but their roofs seem to average out at about five feet). Except it wouldn't be a tunnel; it'd be the residence of a Tock, or a family of Tocks, or a Youth-group Tock Formation—which is what the social statics people call a collection of half-grown Tocks who have chosen to live together. Always in groups of five.

And the tunnel—the residence—would extend off in any number of directions, curving gently to the right here, to the left there, maybe down a little and back toward the entrance. If you kept going in a fairly straight line—following, generally, the widest road in the set of tunnels—you'd find yourself, fairly soon, out on the street again.

And the streets curved, too, for no particular reason: Tocks are not much on straight lines. Everything has a sort of wiggle to it, which may be natural for a snake.

Walking through a Tock house is several different kinds of an experience. The walls glow, for one thing: there are shining surface applications, irregular patches here and there, in all sorts of colors, as if somebody with a fistful of fluorescent-paint tubes had got loose in there and applied the stuff at random, and then somebody else had come along and brightened everything by a factor of ten or so. The patches were almost the only illumination I saw. Once in a while there'd be a room with a small table in it (well, I'd call them tables: they looked like gigantic egg-cups, with most of the upper depressions filled in, and they were made of a material that looked as if it were hardened mud, the color and texture of the very best Earth Carrara marble), and on the table would be a chandelier. Branching sticks, curving out (a large bunch of bananas, standing on the stump of its stalk, if that helps any), with bright lights at the tips of all the branches. The lights looked like candle-flames, and weren't enclosed as far as I could tell. They rose and fell irregularly, brightening or dimming a little for a second or so, though the total light output of a whole chandelier seemed to stay the same; but they didn't waver, and the wind of my passage, and even a little more wind created experimentally by swinging my arms or breathing out heavily at a chandelier as we went by, didn't affect any flame, not at all.

Of course, the whole thing might have been rigged with sixty or eighty separate small fields, one for each flame, optically transparent and so forth, but opaque to sudden airspeed changes. Perfectly possible, but it didn't sound right then, and doesn't now.

"We"? Well, my driver had been told to wait at the outskirts of the city—no cars allowed, which was a perfectly sensible rule for a city consisting of winding boulevards that led into, and out of, the homes of many snakes—but I'd been assigned a Tock guide, a dark-green fellow nearly as tall as Nassanank, which would have made him an even three feet if he'd stood on the tip of his tail, or whatever it was. The guide said he was happy to escort me to see the King, since it was a job that helped him pay off his birth debt. I worked on that one for a while, but I didn't arrive. Apparently every Tock owes a debt to the community for the fact of his being born into it; but whether the debt is owed to the whole community, or to the King, or to the parents, or what, I never found out; my guide was clearly being as helpful as possible, but I was asking the wrong questions. As if somebody asked an Earthman what the religious reasons were for driving on the right side of the road—or the left, depending on where the question is asked; Earth is full of tradition. Or something.

(And what happens if a Tock doesn't pay his debt—whether because he doesn't feel like it, or because he can't scratch up enough non-specific credits—I'll try not to get involved with the Tock economic system, since it isn't really relevant to this report, and since it confuses me even more than the rest of Tock life—anyhow, what happens if the debt isn't paid, the guide couldn't tell me. He did try. "If the birth debt goes unpaid," he said, "then the person can not be said to have been born." That explanation does not, repeat not, translate either into execution or ostracism —I got that much—but what it does translate into is your guess, which is easily as good as mine, and maybe better.)

The Tocks weren't bothered by traffic going through their houses. They had the sort of self-enclosing sense of privacy you find in a lot of crowded cultures: things are seen, but not looked at, so to speak. We just weren't there unless my guide went through a short courtesy ritual in order to introduce me and let me ask a question or two. The questions always left me feeling that the Tocks were slowly being convinced that I was a mental case; the notion bothered me until I remembered that, as far as they were concerned, all humanity was a collection of mental cases. Stealing, after all! And fighting!

My guide told me that the more desirable

houses, of course, were those away off on nearly-untravelled byways; the ones right on the main road, the ones I was travelling through, were the homes of the poor.

God knows what poverty means to a Tock. The places seemed as well-appointed as Nassanank's palace, which was at the end of our main road—except for special human accommodations, which the palace had put in when we'd first settled Haven IV.

And the Tocks I spoke to didn't seem depressed or downtrodden or scarred by cruel fate. On the whole, they were cheerful and abstracted, like mathematicians who had just got engaged to the loves of their lives, but had been struck at the same time by an inspiration that solved the basic space-four tensor and spinor structure.

There were exceptions; mostly, they were expressions, or moods, that I couldn't read at all: they didn't correspond to any human analogue I could come up with.

The city was heavily tree-planted: Haven IV has a variety of shade tree that looks like a giant mushroom with a green, leafy top, and the things were scattered everywhere, with beds of flowers covering the spaces in between. The flowers were red and yellow, blue and white, green, brown, black—every color you can think of, sometimes all at once. Color was the basic fact of the city: between the irregular colored patches that glowed on the walls and the riots of colored flowers outside (all under Haven IV's baby-blue sky), I was a little dizzier when I ar-

rived at the palace than the wiggly wide
boulevards and the varied weirdnesses of Tock
life could account for.

(There were no Towers of London, of course.
There were no towers of any sort. Snakes, even
analogue-snakes like the Tocks, don't like having
to climb up and down a lot. Everything, but
everything, was on the first floor: there wasn't
any second floor. Not even in the palace:
Nassanank's place did seem to have a few more
branching corridors than most, but that was the
major difference.)

Where corridors met, and sometimes where
they didn't but the road felt like turning into a
room anyway, the basic boulevard swelled out
into a roundish node. The tables and chandeliers
were all in the nodes—which I got to thinking of
as rooms fairly easily, and, as far as I know, ac-
curately; so were all the other bits of furniture,
communications equipment, twig bunches (the
Tock version of printed books: bundles of twigs,
each twig carved in a repeating set of patterns,
all bound together in a specific order: a Tock
"read" by walking down the twigs, one at a time
from Twig One to Twig (if it happened to be an
especially long "book") Nine Hundred and
Ninety. The process reminded me of something,
but it took me hours before my brain kicked over
and handed me the association: Braille. The
Tocks used their eyes for colors, and for most
normal visual purposes; for reading, they used
their feet—or their hands; the distinction doesn't
exist, among Tocks)—or anything else a given
Tock, or family, or Youth-group Tock For-

mation, liked to have around. There were a great many 3V sets—"books" weren't on their way out any more than they ever have been in the Comity, anyhow since the Clean Slate War wiped out most of Earth and we started over again, but 3V was giving the old form the usual competition. And there were those odd-sculpture whatsits that seemed to serve Tocks as chairs (or, if especially long or wide, as couches); a Tock bed was more like a large, round object, say a pie plate, with no sharp angles, sloping down to a central depressed part about five feet by three. There were no mattresses or cushions —the Tock carapace makes all that sort of thing irrelevant. Sheets or blankets were fairly thin slabs of the same Something those tables were made out of. They didn't look as if they bent very easily, and the look was accurate: maybe a hard covering slab is what a blanket has to be, for a shelled, or carapaced, race.

(A Medium's bed, by the way, looked almost exactly like a fairly shallow fishbowl. Media residences were always curtained off in the homes of single Tocks of either sex, never curtained for married Tocks, and when you came to a Youth-group Tock Formation you couldn't tell in advance which it was going to be. I gathered that the more modern and daring Formations left their accumulated Media uncurtained, but that the Media were considering going on strike against this. How a group of brainless beings— by any Tock or human test—can go on strike, or even get together and agree to go on strike, I have no idea. And what a strike of Media would consist of is equally dark. They won't wear their leashes when their masters or mistresses take them out for walks? They won't serve as sexual intermediaries? Or what?)

All in all, a Tock city is one long exercise in ignorance, for human beings—ignorance smoothed over by the fantastic glow of rainbow colors and by an occasional discovery that you really do think you understand. It's a very helpful sort of ignorance: what it says is: "Human beings take altogether too much for granted. 'Life as we know it,' no matter who We are, is never going to begin to cover enough ground."

That sort of philosophic attitude is perfectly sensible, but it takes a while to develop. At the time, I was simply piling up one *I don't know* after another, and feeling worse and worse, and more and more nervous, as I went along. When we did reach the palace, and wound through a few corridors to get to the Throne Room where Nassanank—having been politely informed of my visit by 3V as we'd started out from the Embassy—was waiting to greet me, it took me five or six minutes to get rid of the various forms of dizziness I'd picked up along the way, and begin to make sense.

The only trouble was that the problem, as I laid it out for the King of the Tocks, looked to me as if it made exactly as much sense as Tock economics. There had to be a rationale connecting the killings, the explosions, the Crown Jewels . . . in fact, I knew there was, somewhere in the back of my head. But I couldn't dig it out, and nothing Nassanank said was much help.

Queen Jessiss was another matter. Jessiss made sense right from the start, and she very nearly always did. A truly remarkable female; I began to wish, after a bit, that she'd been built in a way that would have let me admire more than her mind.

I have met a human woman who played in the same league with Jessiss. Maybe I have met two, or even three.

Not more.

CHAPTER SEVEN

She came tootling in while I was still trying to explain to her husband why the non-Jewels and the killings had to be connected. Nassanank raised his head a bit and said: "Ah, my dear—" and Jessiss flashed her eyebrows at him and then looked at me.

"You're Knave," she said. The accent softened her voice, I think: she sounded better, a reasonably high alto clarinet, than most human women have ever sounded. She was, to look at, a trifle paler than Nassanank, a trifle slimmer, and about an inch and a half longer. "I'm Jessiss— Queen Jessiss, you'd say, but we don't have to bother with that." She turned to Nassanank. "Has our guest been offered refreshment?"

The King said: "Well—" and I cleared my throat, meaning to announce that I didn't really require whatever Tocks served for late afternoon tea; for all I knew, they ate large purple dragons, live, which breathed fire while being swallowed. (How do Tocks cook, anyhow? One more question I didn't have time for then. I suppose they can handle modern pushbutton ranges; but how does a snake, even a snake with lots of short legs, deal with cooking pots or plates?)

"Many humans seem to appreciate coffee," Jessiss said. "It's an odd taste, but a few of us have become mildly fond of it; of course, we import it from your world of Haven II."

I said that coffee would be fine, and Jessiss turned round and put her head out of the room into the far left corridor, the one she'd just come out of; she said something in Tock, a collection of hisses, clicks, whistles and a rustle or two, and backed her way out again, turning so that she stood at Nassanank's side, facing me. I swear she was wearing a friendly smile—though it took me some while before I even began to think I could read Tock facial expressions.

"Something will have to be done about you humans committing violence on one another," she said, in a crisp, no-nonsense tone. "We can live nicely enough with normal human society: it's quite different from our own, but our young can accept that. This sudden increase in violence, however, is out of the question: it provides a bad structure of stimuli for the young—and even for some others who have matured or aged." She smiled at me again. Nassanank, I think, is a great man—well, a great Tock—but it took me a while to find that out. I was sure that Jessiss was a great woman inside of thirty seconds. "What plans have you made in this area?" she asked me.

"Well," I said, in as reasonable a tone as I could manage, "I'm still trying to figure out just why any of these things have happened. I haven't had a full day, yet, to spend in any digging at all."

"No," she said, a little sadly. "What you have had is part of a day, filled with new catastrophes everywhere you wind. I quite see how confusing it must be; and I believe that the catastrophes have not yet reached an end."

Which was what I thought, too; but God knows I had no evidence for it. "Why do you think so?" I asked her.

Nassanank shifted position a little. Jessiss went on: "Because no structural pattern has yet emerged."

He had a comment on that one: "No structural pattern you can perceive, perhaps," he said —not too mildly. Nassanank, after all, ran the place, and he knew it, because Jessiss told him so. The unquestioning confidence of his tone, throughout, told me that he was one of the happy husbands, convinced he was head of the show. The unhappy ones have been unlucky enough to trip over the truth of the matter— which may be one of those little things that explains why I have never found myself married. At any rate: "Nothing you perceive," he was saying, "but how sure can you be that human structural patterns might not include unknown —"

"I'm quite sure," she said. "I don't understand human beings—no offense, Knave, please! —but I don't have to. This simply doesn't feel right, from any point of view: Tock, or such human views as I can devise, or the viewpoint of pure physical causation."

A woman after my own heart: always go with your instincts. But Nassanank broke in: "Human viewpoints—my dear, how can you even speak of human viewpoints?"

"I say what I know," she told him, not too abruptly, and turned back to me. "Of course this explosion of violence is connected with the disappearance of our Jewels, in some way?"

"It has to be," I said. "The whole thing is tied together: it's all happening at once, and if it isn't connected—" and so forth, a digest of the speech I'd given the King. Jessiss kept flickering her eyelids rapidly, which looked like the Tock equivalent of nodding your head to show agreement.

"Then," she said, "if you find our Jewels, or explain their disappearance, the violence will, at least, return to its usual level?"

"Well—of course," I said. One of my stupider statements, as it turned out. I was going to qualify it some, but the coffee arrived just then, and had to be sorted out.

A single snake, with a flat carryall of woven light metal gripped in two hands, or feet, so that it rested firmly about two inches back of the head: he was our servant. The carryall held a tray, and the tray held three cups of coffee, a very impressive coffeepot, a sugar bowl, a creamer, three spoons and a scattering of napkins. Jessiss said: "Ah," and took the tray and put it on a side-table over to my left. She took one additional small item from it—a miniature coffee cup, with about eighteen drops of coffee in it—and held it while the servant drank. Food-taster? Tock courtesy? Whatever, he emptied the cup, wriggled in what seemed to be a sort of bow, and backed out with his carryall.

"Cream? Sugar?" Jessiss was being the perfect hostess. I took nothing until I'd had a spoonful of the coffee; God knew what the Tocks (or the Haven II plantations) had come up with, and I wanted to be as forewarned as possible. The Queen smiled and took her own cup in a few front hands-or-feet; Nassanank waited until she'd set it down at her side, and gone to get his, which she sugared and creamed as if she'd had a lot of practice. By the time she'd handed him his coffee I was ready for a test spoonful.

"Well," Jessiss said, and smiled at me again. I took in a little coffee, and got a memorable shock.

It wasn't quite Indigo Hill, the finest coffee ever grown; it was somewhere between Indigo Hill and the only coffee rarer than its worth, Jamaica Blue Mountain. Like all good strains, it was clearly an Earth original, transplanted to roomier, even better plantations on new worlds. I'd tasted better coffee, but not often; I reached for sugar and cream, fixed the cup just right, took two long sips and began to relax. Give me good coffee, and you can have—better than half the time, at any rate—any other drink known to man.

Jessis was watching my reaction; her smile hadn't changed any. "I am happy you approve," she said in a perfectly ordinary voice.

I took in a little more coffee. "More than," I said. "You do your guests proud." I made a "toast" gesture with the cup. "But we've still got this whole theft business to figure out—excuse me: stealing. The Crown Jewels."

"I confess," she said, "that I do not understand 'stealing.' Why would even a human being take the Jewels? They aren't his. He has no right of ownership in them; what would make him believe that he had?"

I shook my head. "I have no idea," I said. "But he wouldn't have to have a right of ownership. He wouldn't necessarily care who the Jewels belonged to, if he had them safely in his hands. As long as he held on to them, or was able to dispose of them without too much difficulty, they'd *be* his, as far as he was concerned. Human beings are like that. They even have a saying: Possession is—"

"Nine-tenths of the law," Jessiss said calmly; "yes, I know. Although law is not, in my experience, divisible. But don't you see? That is the point I'm making. There is no way in which a human being could dispose of the Jewels without difficulty: they are unique, and widely known, and your own immense structure of law enforcement must be keeping a very careful watch on possible transactions of that sort. And there would be no way for him to hold them 'safely in his hands'; eventually, a search would turn them up, if it were thorough enough. And I assume that this human being would anticipate thorough searches: surely he knows the value we place on the Jewels, and the value, therefore, that your enforcement armies must place on their return to us."

"Sure," I said. "But—"

"But we return to my question," she said. She

hadn't raised her voice; she was still friendly, smiling. Or whatever it is that her face did that made it seem like a smiling face to me. "What would make him believe that he had a right of ownership in them—even so small a right as the sort you describe—when he can neither display the Jewels nor dispose of them, and when he must look forward to their discovery?"

Put that way, it began to look as if she had a point. "People don't do things for no reason," I said. "The reason may not look sensible at the time—in fact, it seldom does—but it's there. And a human being who'd steal the Crown Jewels would have given a lot of thought to hiding them, somewhere."

"Why would any being want such things, merely to hide?"

Nassanank swallowed coffee, without a noticeable ripple down the carapace. "The thing is senseless," he said. "Absolutely senseless."

"That," I told him, "is the one thing it can't be. To begin with, getting the Jewels at all couldn't exactly have been a simple job. We can start there: where were they kept, and who could have got to them? I don't suppose they were available to anybody, any time—were they?"

"Not at all," Nassanank said, almost snappishly. "They were kept in the Great Hall, upon a shelf of the Central Cone. They were set there to be admired or studied."

All right: I'd see the Great Hall and the Central Cone in a little while. For just then: "How were they guarded? What protection were they given?"

"Protection?" Nassanank asked, in an absolutely blank tone.

Jessiss finished her own coffee. "I believe I see what you mean," she told me. "But you must understand that we do not have your human armies of enforcement officials. A ceremonial guard is posted in the Great Hall, but it is meant only to show respect for the objects within. The members of the guard—all associates of the Royal Household, as I think you might put it— have no enforcement duties; the very word 'guard' is one that does not exist in our language, for their function. But human beings appear to use it for such household servitors. Were some being to reach up and take the Jewels, the guards could not prevent him."

I sighed. "All right," I said. "But at least they'd see anyone who did take the Jewels, wouldn't they?"

"I should think so," Jessiss said. "Perhaps they should be questioned regarding the matter."

I agreed: perhaps they should.

The lovely coffee, once I'd finished it, was wearing off quickly. For a few minutes in there, I'd had the idiotic notion that we were all living in the same world.

But the conversation smashed that notion every time it came to a new turn. I could feel myself getting dizzier and dizzier.

"I would have them called," Jessiss said, "but perhaps you would like to see them for yourself, in the Great Hall? Would that change of status be helpful to your investigations?"

I swear, it took me a minute to sort that suggestion out. When I thought I had it, I nodded. "When can I talk to them?"

"Oh," Jessiss said, as if she were saying the most normal words in the universe, "you can't."

CHAPTER EIGHT

The trouble with the world is that you can't depend on things *not* making sense, either. Jessiss was telling me something perfectly simple: I didn't talk Tock, and the ceremonial guards, or whatever their proper title was—Members-in-Chief, Ceremonial Guild of Respect, Civilization Division, is as near as human language can get to it, she told me a bit later—didn't talk anything else. A good many Tocks had learned Standard, either because their duties required it or out of sheer politeness or curiosity (if the Tocks have motives that fit those names; I think they do, but God alone knows for sure); but most of the race, naturally enough, hadn't bothered.

I think two whole human beings, in the history of Tock-human relations, had learned to talk Tock.

This all got explained to me while we were en route. Once Jessiss had explained the language barrier, and offered herself as a translator, I told her I wanted to interview the guards, or Members-in-Chief, or whatever, just as soon as possible, and she said that "as soon as possible" meant that minute. Or nearest possible equivalent: it may have taken us three or four minutes to wind our way out of the Throne Room and past any number of what I assumed were Royal Apartments, round to the left and back toward where we'd started, up a small incline and down a slightly larger one, and into the Great Hall.

It sat in the center of the Tock city—the center of London—and it was domed. Its roof was aboveground. Haven IV's sun was going down pretty fast by the time we got to that dome, but it still gave enough light to tell me that the Embarcation Building wasn't an isolated freak of fancy. The Great Hall had the same immensity, the same stained-glass feeling to the free dome overhead, the same sense of great scale and total color. The Central Cone, an openwork lattice of wood or some very near local equivalent, that went up raggedly to about my height (six feet, even), was dwarfed; so were the other things lying around, on tables, in protective small domes of their own, or on the floor and fenced off with ropes that lay on that floor. I paid as much attention to them as I could—because any piece of information may come in handy, and because my uncomfortable feeling regarding the Tocks (nice people, lovely people, but I didn't understand a thing) kept growing. It wasn't much attention; Jessiss snared one of the two Tocks stationed in the room and had a rapid burst of conversation with him in the Tock clicks and whistles and so forth. They came over to where I was standing, taking in whatever I could: Tock "books" in that domed case over there, and what seemed to be paintings of different Tocks, all arranged in a beautifully precise rectangle, over there on the floor, and—

Jessiss introduced me to the new Tock—a short, fat male with a distinct wheeze. This one was nearly black, and painted with red and yellow stripes that went vertically from the back of the head about a foot down toward the tail. His companion, I noted, was a light green, with the same painted stripes: badges of authority, or uniforms, or the like, I imagined. (Not to leave the loose end hanging, that's what they were, according to Jessiss and Nassanank—much later, when we had time for a chat.) The short, fat Tock seemed uncomfortable; he was fidgeting with his feet-or-hands, squirming a little, constantly. Might have been the presence of his Queen. Might have been the presence of a strange human being, but I doubt that: he was used to strange human beings.

Partway through the interview (Jessiss made a cool, rapid translator, and—having met Jessiss —I had no doubts as to her accuracy), I began to feel like somebody in a 3V detective epic, collecting clues and girding himself up to say "Aha" when he had enough of them, or when the audience had enough of him. The thing was, after all, a classic sort of detective puzzle, in one way —if you ignored motive entirely, you could look at it as a sort of locked-room theft.

And I don't want to sound like a 3V detective —I have enough trouble as it is. So I'll skip word-for-word reporting of the interview, and squeeze things into a digest of highlights.

Name (to begin with): Kass Kass. I hadn't known that Tocks owned first and last names like humans, but Jessiss told me that some did, and some didn't. It was, apparently, optional and of no particular significance—like (I thought, my mind still spinning a little) aging, or maturing.

My God.

Duties: to watch and cherish the symbols of society that resided in the Great Hall, for half of every day, five days out of every nine. He and his partner would be relieved around midnight, I was told, by a new crew; and, on the four days he wasn't on duty at all, another Member-in-Chief of his Guild would take his post. I collected the names of all these Tocks, sixteen in all. I see no reason in the world why I should bother you with them.

Method of protection of the Crown Jewels and other valuable objects: well, that one made for a little trouble, because "protection" meant several different things to Kass Kass, none of which was what I'd meant when I'd used the word. At long last, he informed me that the Central Cone wasn't domed (which I had, as it happens, noticed), and that the Jewels had been protected by their aura of respect.

It didn't sound as hard to get through as your average bank vault. All the same. . . .

"Who has permission to enter this room?" I asked.

The answer came in sections. Section A: Any Tock, any time. Respect, reverence and knowledge were the purposes of the exhibition, along

with something I couldn't quite make sense out
of, regarding reawakening the Medium jointly
cared for by a male and female Tock, and therefore somehow encouraging work toward the next
generation of Tocks.

Section B: Human investigators—sociological
statics people, mostly, busily working away on
more and more detailed descriptions of Tock life.
I took down those names, too, or at least filed
them in my head, along with:

Section C: "Other humans." For Tocks, humans came in two categories: military (uni-
formed) and civilian. Either could come in and
look at the collection. There were few restric-
tions, the only one that counted being the re-
quirement that any human have his visit okayed
by the King, the Queen, or someone high
enough up in the Royal Household. (The sociological statics people had permanent passes. "It
would seem such a bore," Nassanank said, "to
have to permit them, individually, each time
they appeared. If it became clear to us that a
human being was making a regular habit of his
visits, he acquired a permanent pass.")

One more question:

"If someone had just walked up and taken the
Crown Jewels, would you have noticed? For that
matter, would you have done anything?"

Reply: they'd have noticed, all right. That
was their duty. They were in consciously chosen
rapport with the symbols in the Great Hall, I
was told; what that seemed to mean was that
they'd notice any one being touched, let alone
lifted off its shelf and spirited away. Jessiss told

me, quietly, that the rapport wasn't one hundred per cent dependable ("Nothing is," she added, which gave her an extra ten points in my book, because nothing is, and damned few people seem to know it), but it was better than fair: perhaps ten per cent of the time, one of the Tocks on duty wouldn't notice an object being touched. Perhaps two per cent of the time, he might not notice it being spirited away, unless he just happened to be looking at it at the time.

A two per cent failure rate seemed the Hell of a lot better than usual, unless you're talking about spot-check machinery. And the chance that *both* Tocks, at the same time, would fail to notice the Jewels being lifted brought that two per cent down to spot-check machinery level—say a tenth of a per cent. Which was too damned small to consider.

As I say, a locked-room problem. Hand me my pipe and slippers, Watson, and just a small beaker of LSD, or whatever it was Sherlock Holmes was hooked on.

But there was an out.

Sometimes, Jessiss told me (after a few more questions of mine had got unhelpful replies from Kass Kass)—sometimes, one of the Tocks posted to the Great Hall would leave it, for a stroll. The reverencing was a strain, as near as I could figure it out, and once in a while he needed a little time to breathe and just wiggle around.

Which left one Tock to guard, or reverence, the Jewels—which brought the odds back up to a slightly more reasonable two per cent again.

The only catch was this: nobody, Tock or human, could predict just when, or just what, a Tock would fail to notice. And nobody could predict just what a Tock would feel like at any given time—when he'd be ready to recharge his batteries with a small stroll out of the Hall.

"All right," I said, "the damned thing was just about accidental. It happened, that's all: somebody saw his opportunity, right then and there, and took it. He grabbed off the Jewels on the spur of the moment, on an impulse."

But I said it to myself, so as not to appear simple-minded. It'd be one Hell of a spur, for any moment whatever, that would have led to everything else that had been happening.

Well . . . I had some other ideas. The fact that a small flock of human beings was studying all aspects of Tock existence felt like a fact I could use. . . .

But I had to find out what was happening back among the humans, first. Nassanank led the way round to the Throne Room again, showed me an alcove to the right behind the Thrones, and slid a panel aside, displaying a full visual phone.

No chair—naturally. And the phone was a little below the level of my waist. So I thanked the King and Queen for a fascinating afternoon and early evening full of incomprehensibility, and squatted down to start making my calls.

Just, as it turned out, in time.

CHAPTER NINE

I called the Embassy first off—and got, to my dismay, Betty Gorgial. "We need you back here at once, Knave," she said, after the shortest possible greeting.

The woman got my back up; but I had a job to do, and she seemed to be sitting in the middle of it. "Why?" I said.

Her face got very stern, as if she were lecturing a small child. "Knave: we've hired you. You have no right to question our orders."

Oh, God. "First of all," I said, as calmly as possible, "you aren't a 'we,' you're a Miss Gorgial. Second—"

"Ms," she said.

"Sorry. Ms. Second," I went on, and I don't think my tone or my face changed at all, which is a small triumph, if you collect small triumphs, "second, whoever hired me asked me to do a job —and I don't do that job by following orders, yours or anybody's. I do it by going where I think I ought to go, and doing what I think I ought to do."

She stared at me as if nobody, in her entire life (possibly thirty years, though it is hard to believe that any human being could grow up to be Betty

Gorgial in only thirty years), had ever spoken to her that way. After a second she actually said: "Hmmph," which you don't hear being said very much. I filed it away under Curiosae. "If you just go along, your own way," she went on, "then what have we hired you for?"

Well: "To do a job," I said. "To survive—to help you survive, one way or another. It's my profession; it isn't yours, you're too busy helping run a Consulate."

"But—"

I was making it as short as I could. "If you knew how to do my job," I said, "you wouldn't have had to hire me in the first place. And—since you don't know—you're just going to have to let me do it."

She didn't like that. Not at all. I had the strong feeling that, somewhere behind her eyes, she was planning a small feast at which I was going to be the main course and the Dish of Honor, to take place as soon as her little problem was taken care of.

But, of course, that problem had to be taken care of first. "You asked why?" she said. I nodded at her. It occurred to me, wildly, to wonder what Nassanank and Jessiss were thinking of the conversation—sure, the alcove looked like a full-privacy booth, but does an Absolute Monarch have a full-privacy booth, for *other* people, in his Throne Room?

Revision: does a *Tock* Absolute Monarch—and so on?

Damned if I know. And it didn't seem to matter; whatever they thought of the talk (if they thought anything), the Tock King and Queen already had an opinion of humanity that was, undoubtedly, as peculiar as humanity's opinion of the Tocks. One call wouldn't change that much.

Meanwhile: "I asked why," I told Gorgial.

"The Army is on the edge of revolt," she said flatly. "Supernumerary General Willis has declared himself leader of the entire force on Haven IV. Lieutenant-General Roven—Tal's successor, in the normal course of events—is gathering loyalists—"

"Wait a minute," I said. "*Who's* declared himself Army leader?"

"Supernumerary General Willis," she said. "Really, Knave—"

"And 'Supernumerary General' means what it usually means?"

"Well—of course," she said. "But—"

"Don't go away," I said. "In fact, don't go anywhere. And tell everybody else to wait around, too—especially Chan Benson. I think I want to have a nice, long talk with Chan Benson."

"Knave—"

"I'll be right there," I said.

So much for the safety of London. A fairly large piece of my locked-room puzzle had fallen into place: I was beginning to get an idea of just how the theft of the Crown Jewels had been managed.

Of course, I still had no notion of *why*. . . .

Well, I thought, it might come to me. Meanwhile, stopping Supernumerary General Willis was clearly the first order of business, and I had to be back in the Embassy, or somewhere in the human settlements, to begin managing that.

Nassanank murmured some polite regrets. Jessiss wanted to know what was so urgent—not that she was objecting, but she was curious: what had pushed me into leaving in such a mad rush?

I told her about the Army takeover. She blinked, one eye at a time: it was a Tock expression I hadn't seen before, but I took it as concentrated thinking. She said: "Supernumerary General?"

"Right," I said.

She nodded, the way Tocks nod. "I have interested myself in human organizations," she said. "Of course: I see. You must leave at once."

Amazing woman. "Right," I said again. She turned to Nassanank and told him something in Tock, and Nassanank swayed to one side of his Throne, which activated a little bell. In a few seconds my guide was waiting for me.

"So," Jessiss said, "you will now be able to return the Jewels."

Well, nobody gets everything right. "It may not be quite that simple," I told her. "In fact—"

"Remain peaceful," she said. "We are sure that you will do everything within your power. No more can be asked of any living being."

I felt as if I were backing out of an audience with Queen Victoria, if that's the one I mean. We are not amused—that one.

Amazing woman.

CHAPTER TEN

I started back toward the Embassy. Midway, a better notion hit me, and I asked my driver if the car—or tank, or whatever it was—had a working GP phone. "Naturally," he said, as if I'd asked him whether the thing had a steering wheel, and I told him to find Lieutenant-General Roven and put through a call.

"He's likely to be busy," I said. "In fact, he's likely to be so busy he won't be easy to find by phone. But find him—patch me in, wherever you get him—and introduce me by telling him I'm his support team."

"His what?"

"Support team," I said. "I'll explain some other time: but find him."

A reputation, once in a while, is a handy thing to have. Both the Haven II Embassy and the Haven III Consulate had got together to hire me, sent me a space-four message (which is neither cheap nor easy), and come to the Embarcation Building to meet me. I could assume that word had got round, here and there.

And Gerald Knave: Survivor was a fairly potent reputation to wave around. It struck me that what the human settlement on Haven IV had, in fact, tried to do was to go up against the thief, the enemy, whoever the Hell he was, Knave in hand—as if I were a brand-new weapon, and brandishing me would strike fear into the hearts of Evil Types. Well, it doesn't work quite that way, but brandishing my own reputation—Knave, so to speak, making a foray with Knave in hand, just to see how many Evil Types he could strike fear into the hearts of—might turn out to be very useful. And there really wasn't the Hell of a lot of time.

The bell that kept tolling, all the while I was on Haven IV, was that there wasn't any time: everything kept happening at once. It takes even more getting used to than I've had, here and there.

Nevertheless, there wasn't. These scientist chappies can come up with some perfectly awful surprises, in what amounts to no time at all, and if Willis or one of his group had a brand-new notion for a weapon it would be shoved into the breach before I had time to find out what it was —unless I rushed things.

Oh—scientist chappies? Sure: the science-and-technical corps of any Comity force has Supernumerary for a title: Supernumerary Sergeant, Supernumerary Lieutenant First Grade, Supernumerary Major, and so on up to the top. The word doesn't irritate them: they're proud of it, generally. They're supernumerary to an Army—sure they are; they don't dirty their hands with the fighting.

They just provide the fighters with the necessary tools to bash other people with. This strikes me as a distinction without a difference: if I hand you a beamer and you use it (as I know you will) to burn somebody to a very small crisp, am I any less a killer than you are? But the Supernumeraries seem to have a different attitude. It's all pure science, and if it happens to get used to wipe out people, or cities, or planets (and, because they're attached to the military, the odds on that sort of thing are high), what business is it of theirs? They haven't got their hands dirty: they've stayed as far away from the action as possible.

But Willis—and, apparently, a small corps of supporters—were changing all that. They were going to get their hands as dirty as possible: never mind providing the Army with neat new ideas now and again, they were determined to run it.

That much had been obvious from the time I heard "Supernumerary," and a good deal more had been obvious, too.

I'd been wondering about humans studying Tocks. I'd wondered if—somewhere—a quiet student had figured out something about the Tock nervous system, such as it is (it's something like eighty per cent identical to human nervous systems; most intelligent races seem to work that way, though God knows it isn't a hard-and-fast rule), and come up with a way to turn it off for a short while. Turn off the conscious part of it, at least; there are a small variety of things that can do that to human beings, the leading gimmick at the moment being a freeze charge from a beamer, and Tocks, it occurred to me, might not be immune.

If you run into a freeze charge, you may not even know it—though you are going to know about it afterward, when you wake up with the grandmother of all headaches. Maybe there was something you could do to a Tock that worked the way a freeze charge works—and didn't leave the Tock with the equivalent of a world's record hangover.

And—if there were—then one of the logical people to have come up with it was a member of the Supernumerary bunch.

That much was no more than vague theory—until I heard the news about Willis. Then it marched up to the front of my head, took a placard saying ONE on it, and waved at me. Sure: Willis' move told me—within a reasonable doubt—just what had happened to the Tocks posted in the Great Hall. Willis, or one of his cohorts—by the way, is there such a thing as one cohort, or do they come only in bunches, like grapes?—anyhow, some Supernumerary had come up with a Tock-equivalent, non-hangover freeze charge. One shot from this theoretical new beamer and the Tocks drop, without noticing that they've done so; you walk in, pick up the Jewels, arrange the Tocks so that they're in the same position, when they come out of it, that they were when they went into it—and there you are.

Maybe a Tock would notice that a small chunk of time was gone from his tour of duty. Somehow, I doubted that: the whole business of reverencing, and so on, looked a little too much like self-hypnotism to me, and if they kept putting themselves into near-trances they wouldn't know what time it was, or what time it was getting to be.

Agreed: it was the Hell of a long chain of inference to pull out of one word. But Jessiss had pulled out the same chain, which gave me a certain amount of confidence; and a Supernumerary trying to take over an Army-in-being was a rare enough event so that it required a good deal of explanation. My chain of inference provided at least the start of that chain; nothing else did, as far as I could see. (Though, God knows, I couldn't see very far: that was the other tolling bell on Haven IV, the fact that I never knew enough, and never really had time to find out. If I had . . . well, damn it, if I had, I'd have been able to do something about Betty Gorgial, not to mention most of the damned Army. But I didn't find out enough until long, long after—on another trip, some good while after the carnival of Haven IV was closed down for the duration.)

Only one question remained, and I was determined to ask Roven, when I got hold of him—Roven, and eventually Willis, and everybody else I could find.

I was beginning to know How the Jewels had been lifted.

I was absolutely blank on Why.

CHAPTER ELEVEN

My driver managed to reach Lieutenant-General Roven, but he didn't patch me in. "The General says he sees no need to talk over the phone," the man told me. "He suggests that you come to him."

Whether the suggestion was a good or a bad idea I didn't know, and my driver's tone gave me no clue. He was just passing on a message; responsibility, let alone judgment, had nothing to do with him. Gorgial, the tank that served for a car, the driver—the more I saw of the Haven III Consulate, the better I liked Haven II. Which was none of my present business.

"Where is he?" I said.

"He's at HQ." The driver sounded just a bit surprised. Where else would he be? I sighed a little, and tried again.

"Where is HQ?"

"It stands for 'Headquarters,' " he said helpfully.

One more sigh. Why wasn't I being driven around by Chan Benson, or equivalent? "Where is Headquarters?" I said.

"Oh," he said, and paused. The tank, or car,

went on rolling. "At the edge of town—the far
edge. He retains control of HQ—of Headquarters—so far, Sir, and he apparently feels it
better to work from there, where his communications net is to hand. Of course, I wouldn't say for
certain that the communications net was his reason—"

"Take me there," I said, and something went
sprung! against the slit that was the rear window.

I asked my driver what the Hell that was. His
answer was a model of calm.

"We are being shot at, Sir."

Wonderful. "Do people generally shoot at
Consulate—ah—vehicles?" I said.

He went on driving: maximum speed, fifteen
miles an hour. We were a lovely target. If anybody had a weapon that would go through the
damned tank, we were no better than slowly
traveling ducks, waiting to be potted. "Not generally, Sir," he said. "Not here. On Haven II—"

"Never mind Haven II," I said. "Are they
shooting at the Consulate vehicle—or at me?"

He paused. Then he cleared his throat. "Sir,
as far as I can judge—and you must understand
that my judgment may not apply, since there
may be relevant facts I do not have—"

"All right," I said. "I understand that. And?"

"Well, Sir," he said—almost apologetically,
for some damned reason— "I believe they're
shooting at you. At any rate, that one shot—"

Something went *spung!* again. Louder.

"Another shot?" I said, as calmly as possible.
That tank was a place it was possible to be calm
in: take away the sound effects, and you'd have

no idea anybody was trying, as they say, to do you bodily harm.

"Yes, Sir," the driver said—equally calm, or trying for it. He sounded a little ragged around the edges: tank or not, he wasn't used to getting shot at.

"Slug guns, too," I said. "Lovely people, whoever they are."

A beamer might have gone *fzzt,* or even *ssss,* but it wouldn't have gone *spung:* that was the sound of a solid projectile rebounding off the outside of the car. The driver thought about it for a minute and said: "Yes, Sir:" at fifteen miles per hour, even keeping an unblinking eye out for traveling snakes leaves you time to think.

"Just lovely," I said. Because if a beam doesn't get through, it just fizzes against whatever shield stopped it. If a solid slug doesn't get through, it ricochets—with, maybe, all sorts of unpleasant results among whoever happened to be bystanding as we went grandly by.

Maybe they were trying to shoot me; but they didn't seem to give much of a damn, really, about who they smashed in the process.

Which was an important datum. I filed it that way: "Important Datum," inside my skull. I had a number of things in that file, by then; my instincts were, and are, good enough to tell me what ought to slip into the I. D. file, so to speak. But they're not good enough to tell me why, and they never were.

It was like the damned theft: I had a handle on How, but no notion of Why. Maybe, if I collected enough Important Data, a few connections would begin happening, and all sorts of answers to Why—to several different Whys—would come out of the woodwork. It was certainly something to work on.

If I ever got the time, of course. Which I wasn't getting. I asked the driver: "Did you get a look at anybody doing the shooting?"

I'd been keeping an eye out myself, just on general principles, as we went down the boulevards outside London, back to the human settlement. I hadn't seen a thing, not even the flash of explosives.

"No, Sir," he told me. We proceeded calmly, at fifteen miles an hour. I kept repressing a desire to open a window or tip up the roof (if the roof tipped open, which seemed doubtful) and wave, like the Emperor of the Comity on a State visit. Somehow, given the local marksmen, it didn't feel like a good idea.

Well, there were buildings, there were trees, and there were the Hell of a lot of shadows and the like: evening had come. Any decent assassin would be competent enough to stay hidden, I told myself—if he were human.

A Tock, on the other hand, was, by nature, more or less invisible. I couldn't quite picture a Tock handling a human-sized regulation slug gun, but, for all I knew, they might have models of their own. I didn't think the notion terribly likely—a race that didn't need more than seventy-five policemen to cover a planet wouldn't come up with much in the way of dedicated killers—but it wasn't actually impossible. And, if you ignore those implausible notions, then some day

one of them is going to rise right up and bite you
on the nose, with fatal results.

We had an assassin, of whatever race, who
was aimed straight at me. This was disturbing
enough, and my brain went into what I fondly
think of as high gear.

I started making lists.

Pollorine. Tal. The receptionist (whose name
I never did get). An unnamed mechanic in a
Consulate garage.

All dead—and all, except that mechanic, from
Haven II. Which might have been coincidence—
Haven II had most of the representation on the
planet, which struck me as a good idea, given the
sample: Chan Benson of Haven II compared
very favorably with Betty Gorgial of Haven III—
but might have been, as they say, a clue. Suppose the Haven III people were trying to knock off
the Embassy, and all of the Haven II settlement?

All right: Hold on: All engines full stop: this
space-four card rejects. I am beginning to be baffled by the numbers game here—this business of
Haven II and Haven III and who's who—and if
it confuses me, God alone knows what it might
do to you. So let's try and get rid of the numbers,
most of the time, anyhow. Words are easier.

From now on, the Haven II people, like Chan
Benson, are the ones who have an Embassy—the
Embassy people. The friends of Betty Gorgial, or
whatever she used instead of friends, won't be
called the Haven III people: they have a Consulate. The Consulate people.

Embassy people and Consulate people. Feels
less confused already.

(By the way—not to add to any remaining confusion—I finally did get to see the Consulate building, some small while after all the fuss was over. The damned thing looked exactly like the Embassy building. I mean exactly. What the Hell do bureaucratic piles of stone do, fission like other low life forms?)

So that last notion—as we return to high gear —reads:

Suppose the Consulate people were trying to knock off the Embassy, and the whole Embassy settlement?

Well, even put in a clarified manner, it sounded all right for about a second. But I couldn't imagine a reason for anybody to try that; and I couldn't even begin to imagine any way that motive could be tied in with the theft of the Jewels. And everything had to be tied in. Coincidence is the answer more frequently than people like to think, but coincidence's long arm just wasn't as long as all that.

Once the second had passed, I threw the whole notion out. My first list didn't mean a thing: Pollorine was on it, and there was no way in the world for anybody to have chosen him: as I remembered thinking, several years back, accidents don't care who they happen to. Pollorine might as easily have been Benson, Gorgial, our chauffeur, nobody at all—or even me.

Query: had the recharge post been loaded on my behalf? Was that a first shot, so to speak, to try potting me?

Answer: no. I also remembered thinking just how easy it would have been for a determined assassin to get any or all of us before we'd hit the Embassy building. Anyone deliberately planning for me would have tried to pot me on the way, rather than arrange an accident that had a good deal less than even chance of landing on my head.

In fact, the accident hadn't been aimed at anybody. It had been aimed at the simple idea of destruction: blow up the post, riddle the car and garage, and maybe knock someone off while you're at it; it didn't matter who the someone was. Any of us—or anyone who happened to be in the garage just then, perhaps dusting off a car or putting on a new wheel—might have been elected: the person who'd arranged the explosion didn't care at all.

Which meant, as far as I could see, that the whole list was just a list taken at random: if it didn't matter which of us got it in the garage, then it didn't matter who got it at any other time, either.

That notion had one large virtue: it explained the choice of weapons. Bombs are very helpful devices if you're a killer who doesn't much bother about who you end up sending to a better world: they're about as non-specific as a one-man weapon can get.

It also, as far as I could see, had one large defect: it left me with a murderer (and, by hypothesis, a thief) who was playing games at random. Maybe, just maybe, Haven IV had a maniac on its hands—a maniac connected with the Supernumerary officers, who'd arranged the theft and then gone on a killing spree, for no rea-

son at all—or at the very least, no reason that a
sane mind could unravel, without intensive psy-
chotherapy and probably a building-full of subelectronic brain wave aids.

(For that matter, if the killer were a simple
maniac, the whole Supernumerary business
didn't necessarily hold: the theft might have
been, as I'd thought very damned briefly, a spur-
of-the-moment opportunity. One theft, three
bombs, one—it struck me that I hadn't been told
just how General Horgai Tal had been killed—
well, one whatever-it-was . . . and three nice,
careful shots—two slug, one beam—at a single
target.)

Damn it, even maniacs are consistent, though
what they're consistent about may baffle you for
a while. Did this one have enough residual good
sense to realize—belatedly, after I'd got to the
Embassy—that I was a major threat to him? He
had to think that: the Embassy and the Consulate both agreed on it, or they'd never have
hired me, and it struck me that there wasn't really the Hell of a lot that the Embassy and the
Consulate did agree on. All right: if he had that
much residual good sense, then he'd have tried
to pot me in the second or so between my leaving
the car, or tank, and entering the Tock city. Inside London I was not a very good target, since
everything was made up of intertwined interior
tunnels . . . and was the dome of the Great Hall
bullet proof? Or would "bullet proof" make
sense to a Tock? "Impact proof," maybe. I made
a mental note. I took a quick look inside my head
and found enough mental notes for a good-sized

symphony; well, when I had the time . . .

But the maniac, assuming there was one, had left his shooting until I was back in the car, fully protected, immune to whatever it was his slug gun was throwing at me.

That much made sense, in a way: from near the Tock city, he might have been spotted by a Tock lookout, or just by a random Tock wandering round the outskirts—or by my guide, waiting there at the entrance. Of course, he could have potted the guide as well. . . .

But he hadn't killed any Tocks. None at all. Even during the theft of the Jewels, when the death of two Tocks would certainly have made his life a lot easier, he hadn't killed any.

Just human beings. And almost entirely (by whatever coincidence: I didn't want to put much weight on it, because it wasn't going to stand the strain) human beings from Haven II. Embassy people.

Two beakers of LSD, maybe. Or something stronger. I would have loved to conjure up the shade of Holmes himself for a chat. But even the most dedicated idiot of a medium—a human-type medium, I mean, though the intelligence level doesn't seem to differ much—wouldn't try casting about in the waters of the Great Beyond for a character who was no more than a selection of marks on paper.

God damn it, by the time my driver wheeled into the Embassy garage—no further shots—I was in a perfectly classical brown study. By no means my usual mood.

CHAPTER TWELVE

In fact, it took me fully five seconds to realize that we were in the Embassy garage.

I said: "Wait a minute—" and my driver turned off the electric, pushed a couple of additional buttons (shields, I suppose), and twisted round in his seat to look at me.

"I have received orders to bring you here," he said. "General Roven has been informed: he will await you at HQ as long as possible, and if he is forced to vacate that location he will inform someone in authority here of the fact, and advise us as to any new location in which he may meet with you. But Ms Gorgial—"

So much for brown studies. I noticed, though, that the driver was wearing an ear-bead: that meant private communication, and even if I'd been paying full attention I might not have heard a thing. I sat there with my mouth open for a full second, telling myself not to bite the driver. Clearly, it wasn't his fault: Consulate people, it was becoming sadly obvious, did as they were told, and he'd been told.

All right. "Are you now in contact with Ms Gorgial?" I said.

He reached up to his left lapel and fiddled

with something under it. Right: the ear-bead was his link back to his superior officer. In a bit he said: "Yes, Sir. She wishes you to meet her at—"

"You tell her," I said, repressing still one more desire—this one, to tell Ms Gorgial where to put her damned orders, her damned ideas, and the whole confused job— "you tell her to meet me right here, in the garage. I am staying put inside this car; she can come to me."

"But—" he began, and then shrugged. I could see his throat move, but couldn't hear a word: subvocalization, either into a microphone taped to his neck or an implanted job; and I wouldn't put it past Haven III to plant microphones in everybody under a given rank.

His throat wiggled, and then he sat and listened, and then he said: "She refused, Sir. She reminds you that you told her it was not safe to venture out, even as far as the garage; and there has already been one killing in this garage."

"Exactly," I said. "Now, you tell Ms Gorgial —you tell your God damned gorgon of a boss—" and I hoped his mike was picking up outside noises, like me, as well as his own subvocalizations— "that the lack of safety is what I am working on. There is no way, repeat no way, for me to talk with her until I have been able to talk with General Roven. After that—perhaps a long while after that, since I have no idea who else I'll have to see, or what else I'll have to do: I don't have the information to figure that out, and only General Roven can give it to me—we can arrange a safe meeting. Until then, no meeting is safe. No place is safe. She's in the safest spot I know about right now, and there is no safe way either for me to get to her or for her to get to me. If she wants to find a safer spot, then she is going to have to let me figure out where one might be —and that means letting me gather up enough information to do the figuring." I took a deep breath; that was a longer speech than I'm used to making. "Got all that?"

He said: "Yes, Sir," this time without any hesitation, and his throat started to wiggle again. My brown study beckoned, but I kept it at bay and waited. In a little while he turned to me.

"Well?"

"Ms Gorgial says, Sir," he began, a little nervously—I suppose he wasn't used to people defying authority, and I'd given him rather a large dose of it, just driving back from London— "she says that, if you are insistent on the point, then I am to bring you to HQ. She says that it is not safe for her to come to the garage, and that you should not have suggested it."

I sighed. "Right," I said. "That's what I told her." He looked at me, totally baffled. Subtlety didn't seem to be his strong point. But his throat wiggled again, he asked me if I still wanted to get to HQ (and he told me again that it meant Headquarters), and, when I told him that it was my dearest wish, he pushed some buttons, started the damned tank, and maneuvered us out of the garage.

I compared them: Betty Gorgial and Queen Jessiss. Score one for the Tocks, I thought, and then: the Hell with it, score ten. Maybe a hundred.

"But keep in contact with your boss," I told the driver, as we headed out along the street. "If anything happens among the Embassy people— or if anything at all happens that I ought to know about, which means anything at all out of the ordinary—she's to inform you at once, and you'll tell me. Right?"

Wiggle, wiggle. "Yes, Sir." And on we went. The human settlement wasn't very large, but at fifteen miles an hour, minus stops for red lights, slowdowns for yellow lights, and the like—oh, yes, Haven IV had an entire traffic system, for the same obvious reasons that it had its speed limits and Draconian traffic laws—it took a while to get to the far edge of it, where HQ was supposed to be.

About four minutes in, I told the driver: "Ask Ms Gorgial how General Tal was killed." If he'd been erased by a bomb, too—a bomb that might have wiped out anybody who happened along— then we really did have a murderer-by-chance on the loose, and possibly a simple maniac.

I hate maniacs: they're harder to pin down and put a net over than most people, because they're not even as predictable as the rest of us are—given that we're not all maniacs, which is open to question. Nobody is entirely predictable, but your average maniac is a little too much of a good thing.

The driver did his wiggling-throat act—either the mike was rigged so that he could only operate it subvocally, or else habit was just too strong to break: why not ask her so I could hear?—and said: "She is inquiring, Sir."

I hoped she was inquiring of Chan Benson. I had developed a fair amount of faith in that chubby little man, everybody's kind uncle, more or less by contrast with the insanity around me: if anybody knew, I thought, it would be Benson.

But I didn't find out who she'd asked. In something under a minute—faster than usual for the answer to any non-obvious question—the driver said: "He was shot, Sir, according to report. Ms Gorgial has not seen the body, and cannot testify of her own knowledge—"

"All right," I said. "Okay. I know she hasn't seen the body: she hasn't been anywhere it might turn up. At least, I hope she hasn't." I collected a few stray thoughts. "Does she know what he was shot with, or where he was when he was shot?"

"Yes, Sir. He was shot with a Winchester Magnum rifle, or a slug weapon of comparable force and size—" There isn't one; but apparently neither he nor Gorgial was going to lay claim to familiarity with every known slug weapon— "on Avenue Sixteen, or Shallman Avenue."

"Can you find out which one?" I said.

He sounded reproachful. Even the back of his neck looked reproachful. A long, thin, somewhat red neck: he was a true redhead, one of the very few I remember seeing anywhere. What with one thing and another, there aren't very many people around who even look like pure physical-type breeds these days—I don't, if it matters—and that particular breed seems to be rarer than most. At any rate: "They're the same place,

Sir," he said. "We call it Avenue Sixteen. The
Embassy prefers to call it—" and his tone sank
into superiority at such childishness—
"Shallman Avenue. Wycliffe Shallman, Sir, was
one of the early settlers of Haven II, and one of
the first to establish diplomatic relations between that planet and Haven IV."

I sat still for the history lesson: it might, I told
myself, come in handy. (As it happens, it never
did—or, to be strictly accurate, it hasn't yet. But
you never know.) "And where is this Avenue—
whatever you call it?" I said, when he'd finished.
"Near the Embassy?" It seemed a likely guess:
the exploding post, the exploding desk, had both
happened there. And I'd been shot at while driving back to the Embassy—though I hadn't
known where I was being driven to at the time.

"No, Sir," he said. "It is one block away from
HQ. We are now approaching the Avenue. General Tal was shot one square away from our
present position. Do you wish me to turn here,
and drive down Avenue Sixteen until we reach
the spot?"

Good Lord. "By no means," I said. Assuming
we had one killer on our hands, he could very
well have tried both shots at me on the way to
the Embassy—at fifteen miles an hour, he *could*
have kept up with us, if he were reasonably fast,
and if we hit just enough stop lights and so forth
—and he might still be on the trail.

"Very well, Sir." The damned tank went on
for one more square, and there was HQ: a good
deal of barbed wire, laid more thickly than I'd
ever seen it before (against Tocks, of course, who
could wiggle through ordinary human barbed

wire courses without even a scratch, if they were reasonably careful), and behind it the local equivalent—close enough so that it looked entirely Earthlike—of Arctic weather grass, and in the center of the grass a squat, square building with heavily screened windows, two stories high. The thing managed to look, even at first sight and from that distance, as if it were made out of solid stone five feet thick.

And it was all window dressing—or, rather, material to fall back on if all the subelectronic gear went dead. There'd be a screen—a subelectronic job, I mean—in front of the barbed wire, and a screen blanketing the building, and for all I knew a screen covering the grass. Standard military protection, for one thing; for another, if there hadn't been, General Roven wouldn't have been in there for thirty seconds. Any determined group, especially an armed semi-military group, which was a fair description of most Supernumerary forces, would have made wasteland and rubble out of wire, grass, building and all in the first pass. But a good subelectronic screen might hold for virtually any amount of time, if you were careful about the air you let in (and most such screens have controls that let you be careful).

That is, it might hold—unless you were up against a group of reasonably inventive scientists —which is another fair description of a Supernumerary force.

It struck me that I'd better get to General Roven in a hurry. As usual, it didn't look as if I had a great deal of time to spare.

CHAPTER THIRTEEN

We drove up to the front gate, and my red-headed driver held a square of plastic, or paper, or something, up to the driver's window. There were two guards at that gate, both armed with—I noticed with very little surprise: it's not a standard weapon, exactly, but there are a lot of them in military forces throughout the Comity and outworlds—Winchester Magnum rifles.

Maybe it meant something. I watched one guard (a stocky man who looked as if he had bad breath and too much unwashed black hair—in parade uniform or the like: shining braid and a few medals and buttons draped as carefully as possible over the sagging little man) examine the square—some sort of entrance ID, obviously—with enormous care. It took him about four minutes, which is the Hell of a long time to watch somebody look at an ID square. Then he stepped away from the tank—taking no chances —and I watched his throat go wiggle, wiggle.

Same deal: ear-bead communication, and sunken mike.

Offhand, I'd rather have a phone to hand: if it rang, I'd have some choice about picking the damned thing up. Most phone calls mean trouble, anyhow, though I seldom avoid one, trouble being what people pay me for, among other things. But taking it on is my choice; with an ear-bead, you don't have any choice at all. The thing doesn't even buzz, let alone ring: it just begins to talk to you. Or (in a very few factories, back in the Home Worlds and elsewhere) it plays soothing music, so the factory won't drive you out of your mind. I mean: imagine spending four, or even five hours, three days a week, watching a dependable computer mechanism paint a rectangle with subelectronic circuitry, and then test it for defect. On and on and on, and all the change you get, during duty time, is the one-in-a-million shot, a machine reject or a machine screwup. Then you fly into frenzied action, according to your job contract; that's what you're there for, because any machine is dependable within given limits of error. Human beings do odd things to those limits; no machine can serve as a final checkout on its own. Twice a year, maybe, it'll pass something no human being would ever have thought of passing through.

The rule is: everybody, and everything, we all make mistakes. But the mistakes machines make aren't anything like the ones people make. They're great on fine detail, but not so good, sometimes, on the broad picture. I remember once—the ten-thousand-reproduction story—on Inoson . . .

All right: I was daydreaming about anything and everything and avoiding my major mission. Because, I told myself, that mission scared the Hell out of me. I wished I knew why.

The guard came back, wiggles all done with and a short period of listening accomplished, and told my driver something. I read lips a little, but the angle was odd; apparently he gave us an okay, because the gate swung open and we went right on through, along a curving path that led to the blockhouse.

(Curving path? Right. A straight path gives an enemy a chance to build up momentum. A curving path forces him to keep changing speeds and angles as he comes at you. This theory has been obsolete for some time—if you really want to go for the place, why not just cut across the Arctic grass lawn?—but there is a good deal of tradition in military service. And just maybe, one time in ten thousand, it'd work out right for you. I am no great respecter of tradition, but I am no hater of it either: it's a set of instructions for survival, as tested by the people who've been here before you and have survived. If the instructions have to be revised, then revise them; but don't act as if "tradition" is a dirty word.)

More chatter, more avoidance. Right. We went on up to the blockhouse, and my driver hopped out and opened my door for me.

I climbed out, unfolding a little—most of Haven IV is built too small, and most cars of any sort are, anyhow—and wasn't shot at. No beams zipped past me, no slugs whined. Not even a throwing-knife. So I followed the driver up three steps to the door (three big, stone steps), and I watched him raise his right hand to knock.

He never got it done. The door swung open.

Instructions from the gate guards, of course: and there were screened windows flanking the big front door on either side. My driver left his fist hanging up there, apparently not meaning anything much by it.

The man who'd opened the door was about five-six, which gave me six inches on him, and he weighed perhaps fifty pounds over my one-sixty-five. He was fat, but compact, set inside his neat uniform—green and grey, if you care, the official uniform colors of Comity forces—like the meat inside a sausage-skin. He had virtually no hair on top of his head, and eyebrows like great white caterpillars. His round neat face was nearly unlined, and he looked to be no more than thirty, despite the bald head and the white eyebrows.

He said one word. "Sir?"

My driver took a step forward. Lots of people do that before they start talking. It gives the rest of us a dependable sort of edge. He may have opened his mouth, but before he got a sound out I said:

"Gerald Knave. To see General Roven."

Military talk. Proper respect.

Well, why the Hell not?

The fat man saluted and backed off two steps. My driver went on into the entrance foyer, and I followed him. The place looked like a gentleman's club, a long way preSpace, that had suddenly been converted into a fort. Armchairs and thick wooden tables and all sorts of guns, cartridge belts and beamer blocks all over the place, and curtains (tied back: barely visible through the screens from outside) of magnificent

thickness and color. I expected what's-his-name
—Jeeves?—to come stepping into the room in
the haughtiest manner possible to a proper but-
ler, carrying a machine pistol and a cartridge
case on the same tray with a dry martini. "Will
that be all, Sir?" "No, Jeeves: you might bring
along some cucumber sandwiches, and a selection of freeze grenades for dessert." "Very good,
Sir."

The room covered the ground floor side to side
and about halfway toward the back, as nearly as
I could estimate. It ended, back there, in a thick
brownish wall with what looked like real glass
doors set into it at the middle. I hadn't seen real
glass in a while: glassex is more practical, sure,
but the real thing is worth looking at. Much sol-
ider and more natural-looking, somehow.

The fat soldier had gone through that
doorway, as silently as a human could walk, and
disappeared into the distance—up some stairs to
my left, I thought, but it was hard to be sure.
Real glass reflects light a good deal more than
I'm used to, and the visibility wasn't all that
wide. My driver stood more or less at attention,
six steps inside the room, while the front door
shut by itself (and locked: I heard the teeny click
of a good automatic, probably a Webster). I took
some more steps, and a good look around.

Guns and armchairs. The weaponry wasn't
anything new. And it was strictly small scale
stuff: no atomics at all, of any kind. No sense
blowing yourself up while trying to erase an enemy force on your doorstep, and even the smallest
atomic device isn't all that selective. The

armchairs looked luxurious enough to be real leather; I poked at one and it squeaked, and I sat down, with a small table at my right. I twisted my head and looked back past the side of the thing: my driver was staring at me, horrified.

Military courtesy? I was about to get up— why make an enemy you don't have to make?— when those glass doors opened again, and General Roven came in, with two aides. Very young, very thin, and loaded with documents, walking behind Roven in precise cadence.

Roven ambled. He made a gesture at me and I sat down again; he took the chair nearest to me, found a small table to his left—he was nearly at my side, both of us facing the same way, the far left corner of the room—and came up with an ashtray. "Smoke?" he asked me.

My driver was still looking horrified. They didn't do things this way on Haven III, I gathered. I said: "Sure," and reached for my case of Inoson cigarettes. (Smoking Pleasure Tubes, Guaranteed Harmless. I call them cigarettes. Most people seem to.) I fished one out and stuck it between my lips, and the General, who'd fished out a large pipe and was packing it from an ancient plastic pouch, interrupted himself to lean across and give me a light— authentic preSpace gunmetal lighter, flint and wick, and where he got the fuel for it, or the wicks, I have no idea.

I took one long pull on my red-wrapped Smoking Pleasure T. My driver was still being horrified, but confusion was mixing into his expression.

"Thanks," I told General Roven. He went back to packing the pipe. It looked bigger than he did: he was no better than five-one, or maybe four-eleven, a half-sized version of a man, all sharp angles and quick movements. Grey hair, big grey eyebrows (not as big as the gate guard's, but noticeable), clean-shaven, and in full dress uniform: epaulets, medals, stripes, starbursts, and you go ahead and name it. I wondered, briefly, how he carried the weight of the thing around.

"Hmm," he said, and lit his pipe, and puffed for a minute. The ritual was relaxing me. I began to feel, for just about the first time on Haven IV, as if I had some time to think things out. I took one more pull on my cigarette, and tapped ash into the (glassex, damn it) ashtray.

"You wanted to talk to me," I said.

He spoke around the pipe. It didn't make him easy to hear, but that high, sharp tone is as definite as any I know. "You called yourself my support team," he said. "In what way, Mr. Knave?"

"Well," I started, "you're trying to hang on to a leadership post, against this Willis and his men, and—"

"Please," he said, and the tone turned into a snap. They do that. He puffed on his pipe. The smoke it encircled his head like a wreath, but other than that he didn't remind me of Santa Claus. Santa Clausewitz?

I said: "I've been hired to do a job, you see—"

"Yes, I do see," he told me. "But we haven't got time to talk about things we both know. We haven't got much time at all."

Relaxation left me. Here we were, back on Haven IV, where you had to run as fast as possible to stay in the same place. "I might be able to help you hold Willis off," I said.

"Quite," he said. "But why should you? It's no part of your job, is it?"

I blinked at him. People do get to be Generals by making sense, of its kind. "My job is to find the—" I stopped.

One more puff. "Yes: I know all about the Jewels, and the theft," he said. "It's common talk, in fact, though it shouldn't be. And I know you were hired to find the Jewels, and either return them or make some sort of restitution."

"Sure," I said. "So—"

"But what have I to do with that? Or Willis either?"

"I think Willis may have been involved in the original plot to steal the Jewels," I said.

"And, if he is," General Roven asked me through clouds of smoke, "do you think that helping to hold him off, now, will be of any sort of service to you? The Jewels will remain stolen. Perhaps if he were Commander-in-Chief here instead of myself, you might find it simpler to deal with him about such matters: as one powerful human being to other powers, he might be induced to return the Jewels. Surely he has no use for them."

"That's my trouble," I said. "I know he hasn't got any use for them. Nobody has. So why did he take them in the first place?"

"Hardly my concern," Roven said. "In a

minute or less, Mr. Knave, we shall be under fire. Willis has quite good equipment, I understand: shield-breaking missiles, a variety of explosive warheads, Army-sized beam units meant to nullify a shield—a great many things. If you would like to go to the cellar, I am reasonably sure you won't be disturbed during the battle. Afterward, we can resume our talk—or, of course, you can begin to treat with—with this Willis person." It was the first sign of emotion I'd caught: not anger, but a sort of dry and distant contempt.

And my job was survival. The cellar looked like a good bet. I kept telling myself that, but I kept hearing myself talk, and I was saying altogether different things.

"I'll join you. I'm a fair hand with a gun, beamer or slug, and better than average with machine pistols and that sort of thing. Not much good on rifles—most small-arms people aren't, and most rifle people can't handle small arms effectively—but if the fight's going to be reasonably close in—"

"It will be," he said. "And I was waiting for you to say something along those lines. Mr. Knave, we have a good deal to talk about—including a theory that explains why the Jewels were stolen. But I could hardly talk things over with a—a coward." That dry contempt came back, for one word.

"I don't like being tested," I said, and began to get up.

He motioned me down; I didn't move. "I wasn't testing you," he said. "I was—laying a foundation for our talk."

"But—during the fight—"

"The main lines of the battle are laid out," he said, "and I am in constant touch—" He tapped his ear— "in case of—novelties of one sort or another. These people, of course, will be very good on novelties. But that will be no more than a distraction: if we move to my second-floor window, which has a fine view of the front gate and the fence, and a window seat to allow us to fire in comfort—we'll be able to talk."

I still didn't know why I'd instantly moved to help out Roven. Everybody had assumed I would, but everybody's assumptions do not cut all that much ice with me. And I certainly didn't know why I'd volunteered to help out with a gun, during an actual battle.

I have been in battles. A good many of them. People get killed. I have no desire whatever to increase my own odds of instant zero by walking into any battle not specifically called for by contract, so to speak.

All the same, what I'd decided made sense. All of it. I didn't know why it made sense—that filing-case in the back of my head was going to have some explaining to do—but not knowing why seemed to be a permanent condition on Haven IV.

Maybe, I thought to myself, Queen Jessiss would like me to be a hero.

At that point I realized that my entire brain had turned into tapioca pudding, and stopped trying to figure things out. I got up as Roven got up, and looked around for my driver.

Nowhere in sight. "Cellar," Roven said, and I nodded. Why not? The fight was none of his.

Nor much of mine, as far as I knew.

But Roven said he had a theory. . . .

I followed him two steps toward the glass doors before the first pulsating whine began, and the room lights flickered.

"Shield nullifier," Roven snapped, and walked faster. So did I. It came to me that I had my slug gun in one hand, beamer in the other. (I go nowhere—well, almost—without at least one, and very few places without both.) The whining got louder.

There was an explosion. "Straight in through the front," Roven said. "Trying to break the shield with an overload, plus the force of explosion." He didn't stop: the words were tossed over his shoulder.

There was another explosion as we went through the doorway. The lights dimmed, brightened, and dimmed again. It was getting very dark.

CHAPTER FOURTEEN

Roven said: "Give me your weapons." I just stared at him.

We were up in his second-floor room, at the window-seat. Down below, through the screen, I could see a small mass of people armed with everything from knives to semi-portable shield nullifiers (three men, or four women, to a nullifier: the damned things are heavy work, even when equipped with wheels), and I could see the HQ shield shine now and then when somebody took a crack at it.

"Use your own," I said. He didn't stare; he only sighed.

"I don't want to use your weapons, Knave—" An especially bright light covered a ragged ellipse on the otherwise invisible HQ shield, just to the left (looking from inside) of the front gate. I wondered, briefly, where the guards had got to, and decided I had more important things to think about just then. "I just want to make it possible for you to use them."

Well, I'd had a confusing day; chalk one up to human stupidity. I said: "Sure," and handed over both handguns. General Roven slid off the window-seat, went over to a desk, and came back with two neat-looking metal cylinders that attached to the bottom of the barrel of each gun, and two small, very thin squares that went on the gun butts. He was humming quietly as he attached the things: self-stick, I supposed, or molecular binding fields.

"They'll come off later," he said, and handed me the guns. The weight and balance change wasn't too much; I'd used guns that had felt a lot stranger. "We call it a No-Go Beam: aim it at your guns, and the attachments will fall off. But, for right now—"

"Sure," I said. "I see. Just took me a while to catch up."

A shield has one enormous disadvantage— even if it's built so that selected quantities of air and so forth can pass through. Nobody can shoot in at you; but you can't shoot out, either.

Stalemate—except for the neat little attachments. They'd been developed (military development: some Supernumerary man a couple of generations back) along with the latest refinements in shields. They were hooked in, by automatic beam, with the shield transmitter itself: when you used a gun to shoot with, the transmitter would automatically dissolve the shield for you, for the very short time it took for your shot to get through.

The computer work involved in that feat is just as fantastic as it looks: as I say, the Supernumerary boys and girls were imaginative and inventive types. The temporary loss of shield as your slug or beam went on through didn't much matter, in practical terms, since nobody from the outside was going to have time to predict when, or where, it was going to be: and once your shot had gone by, the shield closed up again at sub-electronic—*i.e.*, light-speed—rapidity.

No risk worth thinking about, then—unless, of course, those imaginative and inventive people had developed a way to home in on very brief shield loss.

In which case . . .

In which case, I told myself, they'd have been inside the shield and on their way to the HQ blockhouse before we ever got to our window-seat firing location. So they hadn't developed that one yet—unless, of course, they were saving it while HQ ran a little lower on its available ammunition. . . .

All right. I shoved the whole complicated notion out of my way, stared down at the mass of people trying to get in, and took one deep breath. I snapped off a couple of slug shots first; I have nothing against beamers, but I'm more at home with the slug guns.

Shot one hit a determined-looking man trying to shove a nullifier around into position. I think I got him in the shoulder, but it didn't much matter: a Magnum 45 has a lot of very convincing power, and it isn't very important where you hit someone: he'll fall down. The determined-looking man fell down. Somebody else edged around him and took over the pushing job.

Shot two: a woman with a very hot beamer, spraying the shield from left to right, concentrating on the gate. Front-row position, she had. I missed her, God damn it, and hit a short, squat man in uniform just behind her to one side, heading rapidly from one place to another. With what purpose I have no idea, but he didn't arrive; he disappeared from sight.

Roven was doing some shooting as well, mostly with a heavy-duty hand beamer set at max. The people he hit, and the surrounding area, became brief bits of black toast before being blown away by the wind. Who was it said that death is so final? Somebody preSpace, who'd never even seen just how final a max beamer could make it look.

I snapped off a third shot and hit a nullifier, denting it a little but doing no real damage. Maybe the thing went *spung!*, but we were in no position to tell: the beamer's small sizzle, and the echo of my Magnum slug job, would have filled the room even if we hadn't had outside noise.

And there was a lot of that: soldiers everywhere in the blockhouse, shooting, yelling orders or congratulations to each other, sometimes sending up the yell that meant Wounded Personnel. (Oh, yes: even at HQ there were men unfamiliar enough with a gun to manage to hit their own people with one.) And the shield transmitted sound: sizzle and bang, the steady, growing whine of a group of nullifiers, the shouting of the armed mob out there.

General Roven seemed as calm as your most phlegmatic cucumber: he just went on toasting anything he could hit, in a steady stream of shots I wasn't matching at all. My own shooting was raggedly timed, the way most people shoot in actual battle: Roven acted exactly as if he were on the firing range, shooting for points.

Maybe that's what it takes to make a General.

My score was six (four slug, two beamer—and three missess, God damn it, but my neighbor's shooting-gallery calm frayed my nerves a little and put my aim off) before either of us said anything. Then the General said:

"Good shooting."

Mine? "Not much," I said. "Six in nine? My average is higher than that—in battle, not on the range."

"It would have to be—if you're a Survivor," he said. "But on this occasion—unready, shooting long-distance at an odd angle, and with a new man at your shoulder—it's a good deal better than I'd expected. It gives me a great deal of hope."

"One additional man isn't going to do all that much good," I said. He shook his head.

"One additional man, with a good eye, can do a great deal," he told me. And I suppose he'd know. "They're a mob out there—a mob of comparative amateurs, perhaps—and perhaps total amateurs. Every shot that goes home widens the crack in their motivation; every shot that goes home moves them one step further toward breaking and running."

It was a long speech, delivered in short spurts, and interrupted by several snap shots with the beamer. People kept getting toasted. There was really and truly the Hell of a lot of screaming and rushing back and forth, not to mention more shooting of all sorts, out there; it seemed a very strange time and place to hold a calm, casual conversation. But most Generals are a little strange, like top men in any field. The average human being isn't a top man—partly lack of talent, partly an inability to concentrate, I think—in any field: the top men are, almost always, non-average.

Which brought me back to Nassanank and Jessiss. It seemed as if that rule would be true of Tocks as well—of any sentient species, for that matter—though God knows I wasn't sure. Someone like Kass Kass might be a little nearer to your average Tock—Kass Kass or my Tock guide, whose name I never did get. And it might, it struck me, be valuable to find out what the average Tock thought about the Crown non-Jewels. . . .

My mind was doing a good deal of drifting. I wasn't drifting quite so much with eye and hand, though: I put another two slugs where I wanted them, in the front row, and two people fell down. I changed over to the beamer (well, it might give people the idea that we had a slightly larger defense group, up there by the window: most people who can shoot tend to stick to one weapon, and the beamer might look like a new arrival, instead of just a change of pace) and singed a wild-looking man away over to my left. He staggered off to the side, out of action, and General Roven said:

"I appreciate that. Callian Suphernam—assistant civilian head of supply for this base. I oughtn't to be bothered with resentment—this is a professional job, and no more or less—but I confess to it: Callian was a man who owed me a few favors. My thanks for putting him out of the way so neatly."

A good eye for someone else's work. While chatting, he'd disposed of three more insurgents, or rebels, or whatever the Hell the right name for them was. He hadn't missed, as far as I could tell, since we'd started. He took aim once more, and a small, shrieking woman with red hair and exceptionally large and visible teeth began suddenly to give off smoke along one side as she fell out of the action.

"Sorry I didn't leave him for you," I said, thinking of Callian Suphernam. Assistant civilian head of supply. "But—they're not total amateurs, you know. You said they could be, but they're not. It's not possible."

He made a questioning noise. His beamer, or anyhow one of them, located and handled two problems, men standing close together: the second was ash before he'd had a chance to realize that nothing but ash was standing next to him. Death is so final.

Maybe you could call the red-haired lady a miss: he'd shaved her just closely enough to set her clothing on fire along one side. I was trying for that sort of thing myself: wounded rebels-or-whatever were people you might be able to talk to, later on. And there seemed to be a great deal I had to find out.

"They have to be at least semi-pro," I said. "Weapons, for one thing: they've got modern stuff, and a large collection of it. A group of amateurs would come at you with four beamers, two slug guns and the Hell of a big pile of rocks."

"True," he said after a second. Both beamers

went into action, and two more people vanished. "And I must have known that, without adverting to it: I'd hardly have had any doubts about our ability to hold this area against amateurs."

"And now?"

"Now," he said, "I haven't got many doubts. We have a good many weapons of our own, and your accuracy, however imperfect, may be the final necessary contribution."

It took me a second: I was the straw that was going to break the camel's back, said camel being the revolt. I snapped off two slugs in rapid succession, wounded a military-looking man and creased the shoulder of a very short fellow in the front row who was trying to (as near as I could figure) either climb the damned field, or batter his way through it with his head. The shot discouraged him, for a while at least.

"All right," I said. "Tell me about this Supernumerary—Willis. I assume you class him as an amateur."

"Of course I do," he said. "He's a consulate man, like the majority of the army here. I'm Embassy, assigned here thirty years ago from Rasmussen. Like most of our Consulate men, he's very orderly, and seems to like taking orders —if you know the type?"

I knew the type. I thought of my chauffeur, and of Betty Gorgial, who seemed to like giving orders instead. A nice, solid, authoritarian society, Haven III was beginning to look like. Not that I'm fond of any sort of government I've ever run into—Alphacent, which is run by spirit messages from Ancestors (the people who get the messages are simple epileptoid types), seems as sensible as any, and doesn't appear to work any worse. But Haven III was shaping up as something a little worse than your usual unfortunate government.

"Strict, firm, and memorizes the Order Book," I said. Roven gave me a nod, and, maybe as a result, had his first total miss, a beam that went just a bit too high.

To take his mind off it all—and because I was a little curious myself: I'd planet-tested the place, and hadn't been back since—I said: "What's the arrangement with the Saurians now, on Rasmussen?"

He shrugged, and potted one more target. It was very noisy, but our whole talk was taking place just as if we were sitting in a calm library somewhere, surrounded by books and spools and such, with a drink at either elbow. Well, I could do it if he could.

Maybe. "They're still biting," he said. "Mostly, of course, the towns are set up so that a Saurian has something harmless to bite when he gets the urge: a stack of plastic boards, some junk metal, that sort of thing. As of thirty years ago, we were still losing about one person a month, but I'm sure that's improved by now."

"Eventually—"

"Eventually we may have to get rid of the beasts," he said. "One way or another: create reservations for them, perhaps, or something of the sort." Another target bit the dust, or rather became a part of it. My slug gun was running low; rather than reload I dragged out the beamer and set it on high, tight. My first shot fried an ear off a crew-cut gentleman trying to help arrange a damned cannon, and set his hair to smoldering nicely; he forgot about the cannon and began on more urgent action. "Damn it, they're nice people," I said. "Must be some way we can get through to them—"

"If there is, we'll find it," he said. "I'm no fonder of the sort of solution a reservation implies than you are. There are a lot of races in the universe, and we ought to be able to get along with most of them. You don't wipe out intelligent beings—" his beamer took still another man out of the fray, without fuss— "unless you've got no other choice. Unless it's—kill or be killed. But I haven't heard of any communication breakthrough out there; and, sooner or later, we're going to have to do something."

"Well, they are peculiar," I said. "But you'd think—" I caught myself: we were drifting far off course. "Some other time," I said, and he nodded. Another shot, another hit, this one along the side of a rebel in floppy clothes, and the rebel (or whatever) began to smoke with indecent haste. "About Willis," I said.

"He's typical Haven III, and he's Supernumerary," General Roven said. "What else would you like to know?" He paused for a second, apparently to consider the question. "When you think about it," he said, "I wonder: *Is* there anything else to know?"

"Record," I said. "Assignments before Haven III. Anything you can tell me. Gossip. If you ever talked with him, and remember the talk, what was it like? Anything whatever, General: I need all the data I can get."

CHAPTER FIFTEEN

The incursion, or rebellion, or just simple attack, was beaten off before the rebels were altogether dust and ash. A cannon outside finally
began its exercises, and that may have done it: at
any rate, the remaining group broke and ran.
With only two exceptions (in both cases a member of one sex picking up a member of the other;
one man picked up my wounded blonde, one
woman came and picked up a largish man I
didn't recall having seen before), the wounded
were not retrieved, and there was no attempt.
Apparently they just didn't care.

I found myself willing to bet, at virtually any
odds, that the attacking group had been com-
posed of Consulate people. Except for the two
rescuers, who could have been Embassy.

General Roven went downstairs and outside,
and checked out everybody and everything he
could manage, personally; he gave a good many
orders about comforting the wounded and jug-
gling things in general back into shape, and he
shook a great many hands. When he could, that
is: a good percentage of the time he got stiff, military salutes instead of friendly, exhausted and
personal looks.

Haven III. Consulate people.

While all this was going on, and afterward in his office, where we scrounged up some incredibly bad coffee and fair brandy, while the night fell on Haven IV (but inside the base you hardly noticed that: the floods went on automatically, the room lights took over from daylight without specific order, and everything was still bright, if not exactly cheerful), he filled me in on Willis.

Apparently the man was an oddity, born on Haven III: there weren't many, yet, in high positions, because the colony wasn't all that old. He'd been born with an eye to the main chance, and a talent for a variety of scientific esoterica—not really a helpful combination, most of the time, because a pure scientist is a little like a poet or a painter, and makes his money many years after he's beyond enjoying it. There are a few planets that pay heavily for good research types, but Willis didn't know much about that, apparently: Haven III was not big on providing information about other worlds. Somebody might want to leave.

And he didn't want to become what seemed to him a "scientific drudge"—a lab workhorse, doing engineering or applied chemistry or the like, working on assignment and never, never, getting a chance to break out of the routine. Lots of people like that sort of life, and a good many remarkable people have lived it, one way or another, but it wasn't for Willis. Not exciting enough.

The Supernumeraries were the obvious answer. Sure, the regulars looked down on the

whole crew of oddball types; but, then, the oddball types did just as much looking down on
"the military mind," as I've heard them call it in
a very nasty tone, and maybe a little more. Willis
would have a job, and a chance to fiddle around
with ideas now and then, and fairly good pay.
He'd even have a title, and a position that gave
him a little for-certain status; and those were important things to have, if you came from Haven
III.

And the Army didn't look like anything but
the normal way to live your life—not to the average Haven III inhabitant. There were orders,
there were rules, there was some fancy backbit-
ing, and you knew Exactly Where You Stood.

So he joined up. He was an imaginative sort,
and some of his ideas were good: he rose rapidly
through the Supernumerary ranks.

He was unmarried, unattached and generally
a lone wolf. He seemed, according to General
Roven, to be "a very intense type of person."

Most of the biography of Willis, sketchy as it
was, I got from the General; some I added by
deduction either from what he said or what he
carefully didn't say. (Protocol: you don't say
nasty things even about your enemy. The propa-
ganda department can do that, not the Generals.
And Roven was a polite man.) I didn't know
everything I might have wanted to know, but I
felt as if I knew enough. The "repressed person-
ality," as the analysts call it, with great intensity
and imagination, the hard-driving man who was
independent enough to be a lone wolf—I'd noticed the combination of traits before. (Hell, I

owned some of them—but only some, thank God.) If General Tal had been a Washington or a Kutuzov or a Marshall, then Willis looked a lot like a Hitler, a Nero, a Genghis Khan, a Lenin. . . .

When a man like that needs an army all of a sudden, he can get one. That intensity tends to be very persuasive; and there's nothing in his private life to have made gossip spreadable. Nobody knew anything bad about Willis: his private life was an open book.

Mostly, of course, because he had none. But it takes time to realize that, and, for a lot of people, time was what they didn't have: Willis could persuade them faster than they could go away and think about him.

Downstairs, matters had progressed to the clean-up stage, taking care of the wounded—the ones inside first, and then, very carefully, the rebels-or-whatever, because they might have been booby-trapped. The whole set-up might have been a booby-trap, for that matter: Willis, if he was the mind behind what had been happening (as distinct from the leader of this rebellion), seemed to have a taste for booby-traps.

But this time he'd left the wounded alone, and the outside force had really gone. Willis might have been leading them; nobody who knew him had seen him, to swear to, and his wounded martyrs weren't talking. Or he might have been somewhere else—almost anywhere else on the planet—leaving matters to a subordinate. Both of them sounded like Willis; neither of them sounded enough like him for me to make up my mind, such as it sometimes is.

He wasn't among the wounded. Nobody who even thought he'd seen our Supernumerary rebel claimed to have shot him with a beamer. So he'd vanished with the rest, or he'd been somewhere else all the while.

Where? I asked myself. And doing what?

They were fine questions. Lovely questions. So was another one.

Suppose Willis simply wanted to take over command. In that case, he'd kill General Tal, lead his rebellion, and, if he won—

Sure. But what did any of that have to do with several bombs, a major theft from the Tocks (whose goodwill Willis had to have, if he took command at all) or anything else that had been happening? (Well, he might have shot at me because he figured I'd be in the way of his takeover plans. But those shots were the only pieces that added in and made any sense whatever.)

I started to say my farewells to General Roven, and then it came to me: "You called and wanted to talk to me. You didn't want me as an extra gun, however valuable: you wanted to talk. Not only about Willis, or the revolt: you had a theory about the Crown Jewels."

"True," he said. "And my apologies: we've been a little busy." He didn't wave a hand at the chaos around us downstairs, and didn't have to. "However: have you considered the possibility that the Jewels might be used as weapons?"

I blinked at him. The military mind: it makes lovely sense, or none at all. "Weapons?" I said, and tried to think of a way to use a group of small spheres with glowing fish in them as weapons. You could throw the things like rocks, and maybe the fish, or the ecological balancing medium inside each sphere, was poisonous—to Tocks, or human beings, or both.

"I quite agree that it sounds odd," Roven said. "But—consider Willis. A scientist, and an imaginative one. Isn't it just possible—"

I blinked.

"Just barely," I said. "But I won't ignore it."

He nodded at me. "I shouldn't think so," he said, and I made my farewells and picked my way through various sorts of debris to a waiting staff car. I didn't expect my chauffeur to be there, and, sure enough, he wasn't: either he was still in the cellar or he'd had orders to scoot for home base as soon as the battle wound itself down, and I'd have put a fair bet on home base.

Me? His orders wouldn't have bothered. I was Gerald Knave: Survivor. I'd find a way to get back to the Embassy—if I survived.

A reputation can buy you a few things. It can also cost you a few things. The staff car was General Roven's little gift, no more; it was just as tanklike as the car I'd come out in, but somehow didn't seem so oppressive.

I climbed in, and we buzzed off for the Embassy.

CHAPTER SIXTEEN

Willis, I told myself, might have knocked off
Betty Gorgial. The thing wasn't even remotely
probable, but it cheered me up on the drive back
—which was even longer than the drive I'd taken
to get there: the staff chauffeur was even more
careful about Tocks, and never ran the machine
over about nine miles an hour.

They were both Consulate people, though,
and that gave me a ground for thinking that he
hadn't killed her, but was working with her.
Planet mates, and the like.

Maybe, I told myself, and filed it, and did my
best to forget it. Haven III had a lot of representation on Haven IV—most of the army, it
seemed, as well as the Consulate and an odd
shop-owner here and there—and Willis certainly
wasn't hand-in-hand with all of them.

For all I knew, his best co-conspirators (if any:
though it didn't look likely, the thing might just
have been a solo job all the way through, as far
as I could judge then) might have been Embassy
people, though that sounded wildly unlikely.
They might even have been the three or four
Tocks on the planet suffering from one of those

137

strange diseases that made them act human, and steal things.

The fact was that I didn't know enough about Willis. And I knew just enough about General Horgai Tal—though I didn't refer to it, riding along in our cautious manner, which sometimes made me want to jump out and run alongside, waving—just enough so that I could react reasonably when my driver said, with an apologetic tone in his voice: "I think we'd better go round the long way, Mr. Knave."

I began to ask: "Why?", looked out of my small side window, and swallowed the question whole.

The news of General Tal's death had got out.

We were heading down a street near the edge of human settlement on the planet: there were some buildings, most of them one-story, a few towering a whole two stories above ground, and all of them, as far as I could see, shops, at least at ground level. A bakery, a shoe-repair shop, a souvenir shop (souvenirs, tobaccos, and miscellaneous, even including a few tattered actual books), a clothing store, what seemed to be a restaurant (authentic Arthur cuisine, it said: it seems that Arthur is the name of a city on Haven III, God knows why), and—

At that point I stopped listing. The riot was taking place in front of the restaurant, about two hundred feet down the road, at the far end of the street. My driver hadn't quite come to a halt, but he was creeping along, toward that riot, at something less than half a mile an hour. And the riot had spilled out from the building onto the street, not quite blocking us. The rioters were all human beings, all in non-military dress (most of Haven IV dressed in the styles of, approximately, Earth 1930, and ran heavily to semi-formal clothing—suits and ties, vests and so on: the rioters were a mixed bag, with a higher-than-usual percentage of casuals, pants-sweater-and-jacket, and so forth), some of them carried signs, and I could see a good many of them doing a lot of shouting.

Inside the staff car, I couldn't hear them, which was just as well. But I could read the signs:

TAL WILL BE REVENGED

NO HAVEN FOR TOCKS

ONLY HUMANS SERVE HUMANS

NO MORE MURDER: TOCKS OFF-PLANET

And, as they say, so on. The last one especially fascinated me: it seemed to be a variant on the ancient call: "Go back where you came from," and how the writer, or the carrier, of that sign could have committed the thing or even waved it on a planet that was host to a single, small human colony and the entire race of Tocks, was beyond me. It stayed beyond me; every once in a while, I run into a human being whose thought processes, if that's what they are, are just as alien as the thought processes of the average Tock. More so, if possible.

People were getting hurt. Not humans, mostly: Tocks. I told the driver: "Don't go anywhere. Find a parking spot, get into it and stop. I'm getting out here."

He turned and stared at me—stopping that half-mile-an-hour crawl first. "But, Mr. Knave —if you need further information, you can surely get it in a more peaceful neighborhood—"

"At the moment," I said, "I don't want information. I want to stop what's happening. Park, God damn it, and let me out."

He started one more "But," and quelled it bravely. Mr. Knave, he was telling himself, knew what he was doing.

It's always nice to see such faith. He took better than half a minute to park—there were only two other cars on the street, but he was, as the traffic laws insisted, a very careful driver—and I spent the half-minute checking out my weapons. One beamer, max charge; one slug gun, full up again (I'd reloaded and recharged before leaving General Roven, which made simple sense) with its ten shots, and a few more bunches of ten stuffed into an inside pocket.

Weapons checked out: one deep breath: and the car was parked. I heard a small, dull click.

"The passenger door is open," my driver said. "Mr. Knave—"

I didn't wait for whatever cautionary or hortatory words he was going to wrap up and give me. I ducked out of the car, slammed the door behind me with my left—*i.e.*, beamer—hand, and started down toward the damned riot, both guns drawn. Beamer set on freeze: why kill if you don't have to? Dead men are notoriously unhelpful, but the wounded or frozen might give me something I could use.

Walking down, I could hear the damned fools. They weren't shouting anything that made any sense—what I could make out through the word-less yells and howls was about the same as the stuff on the signs—but they were loud, and they were dangerous. Twice, I heard a bat-like squeal that didn't come from any human throat.

They were fighting two Tocks, sometimes grabbing them to throw or to try breaking (Tocks don't break nearly as easily as you think they're going to), sometimes trying to beam them or step on them. (They don't take to being stepped on very well, either: it's like stepping on a piece of steel pipe). The Tocks were making the squeals, either as signals to each other or when a beamer came close enough to singe that outside carapace.

A lot of the crowd wasn't bothering with the two Tocks outside: they'd turned into specialists in window-smashing, table-and-chair destroy-ing, and general wreckage, and they were mak-ing the restaurant into a pile of useless bits just as fast as possible.

It was all beamers: they're the fashionable weapon, and the one most people do seem to carry. And there was enough pushing, shoving and screaming so that everybody's aim was ter-rible: with maybe thirty-five human beings, and two Tocks, and a great deal of beaming, they hadn't managed to do any permanent damage to either Tock.

Unless there was another one, lying underfoot in the mob, whom I hadn't seen. . . .

Nobody noticed me. It was a busy little crowd. Thirty feet from the near edge of the riot, I aimed my slug gun more or less straight up and fired. One shot.

A Magnum 45 makes the Hell of a loud noise.

I won't say that everybody stopped. There was a little continuing motion, of a more or less spasmodic kind. But my one shot was followed by a vast, respectful silence. The damned mob seemed to turn on signal, as if it had only one mind (if that: mobs are not noted for intellect), and fix on me. The Tock who'd been flying through the air, courtesy human propulsion, came to rest on somebody's shoulder and he stared at me, too. The Tock on the ground was invisible, lost in a forest of feet and legs.

"All right," I said, in as official a voice as I could manage—and my visit with General Roven had given me something to imitate—"just what in Hell is going on here?"

The necessary, stupid first comment. Necessary because it sets the terms of discourse to come; stupid because what you get is thirty-five human voices, and two Tock voices, all explaining at you, all at the same time, and all at about the same volume. This chaos went on for a little over half a minute, during which, (a) nobody was doing any fighting (the various small spasms had petered out of their own accord, as soon as the mob action in general wasn't feeding them), and, (b) I could not make out so much as a sin-

gle word from anybody. At the end of this period, I pointed my slug gun at the sky and gave
everybody a shock, all over again. It's an effect
that doesn't wear off for a while: if you have to
do it five times, say, in the course of one
discussion-or-whatever, the fifth time nobody
will pay any attention. But twice was perfectly
satisfactory.

Instant silence.

"Now," I said. "Suppose I get some explanations—one at a time." I looked around at the
mob and pointed at the man I'd picked out
before I'd fired my first shot: a tall, husky human being, maybe three inches over my six feet
even, maybe fifty pounds over my one-sixty-five.
The swarthy type, with a cap of short, curly hair
and a moustache that looked like a pencilled
decoration. He hadn't been actively throwing
Tocks around, or trying to singe them; he'd been
occupied mostly with pushing, shoving and
shouting. "You," I said. "What's your name, to
begin with—and what's happened here? This
used to be a peaceful street—" a safe statement,
since if it had been the scene of a lot of eruptions
it wouldn't have displayed so many ground-floor
stores—"and it's turned into a battleground.
Why?"

His name was Charrin Densmiss, which
sounded as if it had been translated from Tock.
Or from something, at any rate: one of the odder
names I can remember. And he began with
about what I expected.

"They started it. They don't want us here—

they want to kill off humanity. General Tal is dead. And there's been some more trouble: have they told you about the bombs?"

"They?"

"The military—" He stopped. "Wait a minute. Who the Hell are you, anyway?"

I'd given him the cue. "My name's Knave. I'm an expert, hired by the human settlement. I'm supposed to take the humans here out of any danger—"

Somebody else in the crowd—a tall thin woman with red hair and pimples, as I recall—broke in suddenly: "Embassy or Consulate?"

I think I'd expected that one, too. At any rate, I had a solid answer for it: "Both." And then, as the crowd (which was ceasing to be a mob as it began to adjust to not running around, screaming and breaking things) muttered odd questions: "Just like Horgai Tal. I'm working for all humans here."

"The bombs," my spokesman said. "I tell you, they want to wipe out humanity. Do you know about the bombs?"

"I know," I said. "I was damned near blown up by one. I've been shot at, too—long before I got to you." More crowd mutterings. They made a good set of extras, it occurred to me. If only there'd been a 3V setup, or the like: *Adventures on Strange Worlds*, watched by avid billions back in the Comity. I began to think of myself as a 3V star, which is a dangerous frame of mind to get into.

"Well, then?" he said. "They're trying to get rid of us—all of us. And we've got to fight back."

"Here?" I said.

That one word got me a variety of replies: "They're leaders," and "They threw a human being out, last week," and a few more, including, so help me: "They overcharge."

"They aren't leaders," I said when the chatter had died down. "They're just handy—people you can pick a fight with, that's all. And this whole thing isn't—"

"People?" the pimple-faced redhead yelled at me, from the middle of the crowd. I'd spoiled her fun, and she was shrill and angry about it. "They're not people—they're snakes."

Oh, well: relations between humans and Tocks were generally good (I'd been told—by Chan Benson), but prejudice does keep cropping up. If it isn't one thing, it's another. PreSpace, it seems, there was the Hell of a lot of prejudice over skin color. Or hair color, or something of the sort. My redhead would be away out on the fringe of society on Haven IV, with a few equally mad companions; but she wouldn't be alone.

It struck me that I could use her. "They're people," I said, "by the only test that counts: they can communicate, they have intelligence, they have feelings, just like humanity. If we're people, they're people. Let's get rid of the silliness: there are more important—"

"They're snakes," she yelled. "Snakes! Snakes! Wriggling, slimy horrors—not fit to share our world, or use our technology—not fit for anything but extermination! Snakes!"

That about covered it, I told myself. Of course, we were all involved in a discussion that kept including bits of total insanity—"our world," for instance, or the Tock's ambitions to "Wipe out humanity," when they'd never left their own planet, and had no plans, and everyone knew it. (And, as always, even the mad have a little sense. The Tocks, in a good many cases, *weren't* fit to use our technology: the machines and tools weren't built for a race of three-foot snakes. I didn't bother pointing that out, or adding to it that the Tocks had invented most of the adaptations, as far as I knew, that did let them use such bits of our technology as they cared about. The first rule in a crowd is: Keep things simple.)

So I said: "They're not snakes: they're Tocks. And they have brains, and feelings. They're not slimy, and they don't even have to wriggle. You all know them: you've dealt with them. They're the same as we are—where it counts."

Crowd mutters. But, as I said, I thought I could use the redhead, and the mutters sounded as if I'd been right. These people weren't all out on her particular lunatic fringe; and her attack had started them joining me, and defending the Tocks.

I let that go on for a full minute, maybe more. I saw the Tock on the ground wriggle—apparently he thought it a faster method, or a less conspicuous one, than unflapping and using his legs—off to the edge, toward his storefront. Nobody saw him go inside. The one on somebody's shoulder just stayed there. Thank God, he didn't move and call attention to himself. What I wanted was abstract argument, or at least the mood of it.

"And whatever they are—they're not doing all this. They didn't kill Tal; they didn't set the bombs. Humans have done all of that—and humans are ready to do some more. General Roven, for instance—" and I filled them in, using the Hell of a broad, fast brush, on the revolt I'd just come out of, without naming any other names and without giving any motives. They listened, without fidgeting too much. The redhead was talking to a short man next to her in what looked like the Hell of an urgent undertone, and the short man was looking uncomfortable. Great.

"It's not humans," my spokesman said flatly, in large, solid tones. "It's the damned Tocks. They want to—"

"Tocks don't kill," I said. "And, besides that—"

"How do you know?" he broke in.

Well, how did I know, at that? I knew because somebody had told me, essentially. Nassanank and Jessiss, and my whole tour of London—none of that was evidence for anything. The King and Queen might have been perfectly nice people; my tour might have been rigged to show me only the peaceful parts of the city.

And—*Tocks don't kill* was just something everybody knew. Once upon a time everybody knew space travel was impossible, and where did that leave you?

But, just then, everybody was right: Tocks didn't kill. Nothing that had happened since my arrival—Hell, very damned little in the recorded human history of Haven IV—made sense otherwise.

Which was not an argument I wanted to try out on my captive crowd. Once more: you have to keep it simple. "I've studied them," I said. "And I've studied captured Tocks. I'm an expert —that's why the Embassy and the Consulate, both, hired me. Both of them; just like Horgai Tal."

"But they want to—"

"Drive us off the planet?" I said. "Nope. They invited us down in the first place. They've accommodated to our ways, from language right on through diplomacy and armies. They want to get along with us."

My spokesman—Charrin, for God's sake, Densmiss—snorted. It isn't a sound you hear a lot of, for some reason. "Get along with us," he said, "or else study us until they were sure they could make their move, and wipe us out." He looked at me with a perfectly satisfied expression; that was his crusher.

And a lot more crowd-murmur told me that it was the crowd's crusher, too. All I had to do was shrink it down to size.

Right then, it looked a little difficult to shrink. The damnedest things sound as if they make sense, now and again; for all I knew, Charrin Densmiss was perfectly right. If everything I'd been told about the Tocks was wrong, that is.

And it wasn't: it couldn't be. "They're smart," I said. "They have to be—even on your theory, that they're studying us. It takes intelligence to figure out an alien race, and we're aliens, to the Tocks." All of which was perfectly obvious, and had to be said. It was like a debate, there in the street, surrounded by wreckage. The Tock on somebody's shoulder was looking at me with his head cocked, and an expression I couldn't read at all on his face. (Distinctly "he," by the way: it's mostly the shape and color of the shell-like things that make up the carapace, plus some differences in facial arrangement—length, eye size and so forth—but you can always tell. If you've run into same-sex dressing and hair customs on one of the small scattering of planets that is diseased with them at the moment, you'll find it a good deal easier to tell male from female among Tocks than among human beings.)

Densmiss said: "All right, they're smart. So what? All the more reason to get rid of them, before they—"

"Before they what?" I said, making my tone even harder and louder. "Figure it out, friend: the Tocks have waited, and waited, and studied us, all this time. And now they want to wipe us out—at least the ones here on Haven IV."

"And everywhere else," the redheaded woman yelled.

Generally, I like redheads. Maybe that one dyed her hair, and was a natural mousy brown or something indifferent. I held that thought.

"They don't have space travel," I said. "And they don't seem to want it—though of course all the experts could be wrong, and you right, and the Tocks might have been hiding their motives about going offplanet all this time. In which case, of course, they've got our spaceships—"

"They God damn well will, unless we get rid of them!" Densmiss said.

"Sure," I said. "If they can work the things. But never mind that—assume anything you like about space travel. If the Tocks have been waiting all this time, and if they're intelligent—then why in Hell would they start fighting human beings by killing us off one at a time?""

There was an answer. Not a good one, but a fast one; Densmiss had it instantly. "They can't manage anything better," he told me. "And those bombs—that's a good way to kill a lot of people all at once. Maybe it's the best they can do."

"Sure," I said. "But they'd have to know we'd come out after them. They've been studying us, right?"

The crowd was getting restless, as they say. A little stirring, a good deal of mutter. The Tock on somebody's shoulder wasn't moving at all, not wanting to call any attention to himself. For all he knew, for all I knew, the shoulder's owner didn't even know he was there. Tocks are fairly light, and you tend to accept any steady message from your nervous system, even a message about additional weight, by just putting it into file without taking it out to look at—especially in the middle of a mob scene.

But the mob scene was cooling off, and changing. If I left it, before I had it tied down a little, or before some sort of help arrived (I never did tell my driver to radio for aid: that would be automatic, once I'd become a damned fool and left the car)—if I left it, it was going to turn back into a mob again, and fast. And a more savage mob, at that—making up for lost time, as it were.

"Sure they've been studying us," Densmiss said. "God damn it, this is no time for talk— we've got to—"

"We've got to figure out what in God's name we're doing," I said. "Before we do it—not afterward, when all you can do is send regrets if you made the wrong move. And—look at this: if they've been waiting all this time, and if they knew (and they'd have to know) that killing us off one at a time, or even in small batches with small bombs, would bring us out after them— well, they've waited a long time. Why not wait a little longer, and develop something that would do the job all at once, neatly and finally?"

"But they—"

"There are lots of possibilities," I said. "A gas that affects us, but not Tocks: our systems are a long way from identical, even though we can eat some of the same food. Or some form of radiation Tocks can stand, that scrambles human brains. Or—well, there's a long list; I could stand here until dawn and tell you about it, but you don't need that."

And they didn't. There was a lot more shouting, by Densmiss and the redhead and most of the others. Their first idea was that I was helping the Tocks by suggesting new weapons for them, and I had to knock that out: they were intelligent, they could see the possibilities as well as any human being, and all I was doing was pointing out that they *didn't* have the weapons needed.

And wouldn't, therefore, have come out fighting. They'd waited a long time; if good weapons development took a little longer, they could wait a little longer—and would, being intelligent.

The crowd had lots of other objections, and I swear I stood there and argued with them for half an hour or better before I heard the reinforcements arriving. I had them pretty well convinced—calmed down, ready at least to go home and think things over before going on with the spree in progress.

Of course, the reinforcements ruined that. Entirely, and at once.

CHAPTER SEVENTEEN

In a way, it proved that the Tocks hadn't been studying us, not in real detail—or, at any rate, that these Tocks, who just had to run a restaurant, had not done a lot of studying. They had no idea how human beings react to the threat of immediate restriction.

Tell a man he can't spit on the ceiling, it's against the law and you'll arrest him if he does— and he's likely to set a new high jump record for the planet, trying. And get a crowd, lately involved in mayhem and attempted massacre, all nicely calmed down—and then let them hear sirens. The people behind the sirens are coming to stop you, friend, to round you all up and make it impossible for you to go on with your merry career.

Oh, are they? That's the typical human reaction. The Hell with reason, the Hell with sense, the Hell with everything: if these people are going to try to stop me, then I'm God damned well going to try my best to make sure they fail.

Except for special circumstances, the period between the first siren and the instant in which the local police take over is likely to be the noisiest, and most frenzied, part of the riot. If we don't get it done now, we're not going to have another chance, right? And don't ask whether or not we really even *want* to get it done.

They're going to stop us, aren't they?

It seems to be sufficient reason.

And the local traffic laws—sure they're perfectly sensible, but you can find a flaw in any diamond if you look hard enough—made that period, from the first siren to the actual arrival of two large carloads full of police (Consulate, by their no-nonsense uniforms) about five times as long as you'd normally expect it to be.

This left five times as many minutes for the crowd to turn back into a mob, forget all about muttering and trying to listen to my peaceful attempts at debate, and start wreaking any old havoc that happened to be within reach.

Oh, God.

The restaurant had been a shambles. It became, rapidly, the remnant of a shambles, strewn all over the sidewalk, all over the street, and halfway down the block; not to mention the small bits of plastic, metal, glassex, tablecloth fabric (probably more plastic) and general decoration, including silverware and bits of imitation table-flowers, stuck in everybody's hair, clothing and, for all I could tell, teeth.

The Tock who'd been sitting on that shoulder took about seven-tenths of a second to unflap and gather itself and gather itself, fully legged, for a leap. Those short, comparatively thick little legs seem to have the Hell of a lot of power to dispose of, not to mention the advantage any Tock has by reason of the square-cube law: he masses a lot less, and he can move a lot higher and farther.

The Tock's first leap brought it, in a reasonably flat trajectory, over the heads of the crowd, almost too fast to see at all and certainly too fast to notice (I'd been keeping one eye on him, and was watching before he moved—and I think I was the only one: everybody else was just too hysterically busy), and then down to the ledge of his place's broken front window. His second leap took him from there straight on back and out of sight; if he had any sense, he wouldn't let the back door stop him, not just then, and his partner would be going along.

The cheerful noise of total wreckage was in the air. And a small percentage of the crowd—say five people, maybe six: I didn't really want to stand there and count the damned fools—decided that it would be more fun to table the destruction of the store for a small while, and set about the destruction of me instead.

I'd been keeping them from their pleasure, hadn't I? Just the way the cops behind those sirens would do. And I looked a lot easier to take than the cops were going to be: no uniform, and there was only one of me. And not all that threatening, either.

This look is deceptive. But, my God, I didn't want to kill any of the idiots. There had been enough killing already, I thought—in fact, there had been too much. As a general rule, God damn it, one is too much. So I showed my sudden enemies both guns: slug in my right, beamer in my left hand, aimed, cocked and ready.

It reminded them: I'd done a little shooting, if only straight into the air. But that had been enough: it convinced them that I was truly ready to do some more, aimed a little lower down.

The five were bunched up: two in front, both men, and three very close behind—one more man, at my left, and two grim-looking women. I hadn't been arguing with any of them; these were strangers. It's a lot easier to destroy a stranger—most murders happen among people who know each other simply because most motives do.

The display of guns stopped them for a whole second. I moved forward, hit the front man on my left with the reversed butt of my beamer, swiping him into his right-hand colleague, and went round to the left as he staggered and fell, taking the other front man with him: two down, one of them down and out.

In the few seconds before the right-hand front man untangled himself from an unconscious colleague and scrambled to his feet again, I tried the same notion on the leftmost of the three second-row attackers. It was a ragged row: I swiped him and he fell to the side, but he missed the center gal entirely and clubbed the right-hand gal across the back of her near shoulder with one flailing arm.

The right-hand gal staggered forward just far enough to kick the front man who was trying to get up. The center gal was making a good deal of noise, of the *Grr* and *Hai* variety, and I feinted toward her, tilted away the Hell back on my heels as her claws came out and raked air, and dropped her with a fist (wrapped around the beamer's barrel, but the beamer didn't add much) coming in from below, straight into the diaphragm. She folded and sucked air, making, I suppose, the wheezing sound people make when they can't breathe all of a sudden, but I couldn't hear it through the general chaos. I used the beamer, gently, on her head just over the right ear as she bent, and she was out before she began to breathe normally and headed for the ground nose first.

The right-hand gal was still active, and regaining balance fast. I stepped carefully, not wanting to leave any extra heel marks on anybody already out of mischief, and tried that feint forward again, and almost lost my nose and chin. This one packed a knife—maybe she just liked knives: lots of people do—and knew how to use it. I went back on my heels with great speed, and she missed me by less than half an inch.

But she'd taken her cut like a good knifeman, up from under, and thought full arm power would see her through. When nothing stopped the blade but air, it kept on going up, and she was wide open. I hit the side of her head with the slug gun (reversed butt again), and her knife wrist with my left fist, more or less simultaneously.

The knife dropped—harmlessly, I hoped. There were a lot of innocent, unconscious targets down there. The gal dropped right behind it— swaying a little, and, by God, managing to fall straight onto the head and shoulders of the right-hand front man, who was trying to get up again after having been kicked.

It was the final discouragement: he just went down under her, and scarcely even twitched when he hit bottom.

I took a look and found the knife resting flat on the back of the left-front man: it hadn't even cut his jacket. I stuffed the beamer away, grabbed the knife and shoved it into my belt, where it seemed a good deal safer than it might have been lying around. I grabbed the beamer out again and looked around.

Nobody else was trying for me: the store had everybody's attention engaged. Total time, maybe eighty seconds from my first move. The sirens were closer, but not all that much closer.

Well, there was very little I could do about anything from there, and if I had to explain matters to anybody, I thought it might as well be the people who'd hired me: the cops could wait. I ducked back toward my waiting car; after five steps I turned, seeing no further need to guard my own rear, and ran for it.

The driver was waiting for me. As I got there, the back door on the sidewalk side—my side—sprang open, damned near catching me a very nasty blow on the lower chest. I jumped aside, slid into the car and pulled the door shut.

"Home, James," I said over the mob and the sirens. "Don't run us into the police—and don't break any traffic rules, for God's sake—but—please—home, James."

"Yes, Sir," he said. I think he was laughing, just a bit. That tabbed him, for me: an Embassy man, beyond a doubt. On a regimented world, the sense of humor is the second thing to go, right after the large basket called personal freedom.

He started the thing, and we turned and rolled away, on a long detour. Behind us, and around us, I could still hear the mob and the sirens, for what seemed like a long time.

CHAPTER EIGHTEEN

It occurred to me, before we reached the Embassy, that I didn't really have the Hell of a lot to explain. If I were right—and I felt reasonably sure of it, though it made me a little dizzy to look at it for long—I had my hands on the weirdest set of motives for murder, theft and assorted mayhem I could remember hearing about. Of course the dust-up over the Tocks' restaurant had kicked my brain, such as it is, into high gear, and once I began to wonder about that dust-up, the whole wild pack of cards began to make some sense. I won't say it made a great deal of sense, but most things don't: at least I had a working hypothesis.

And for about a minute and a half I was all primed to go and explain the whole thing to everybody in sight: Gorgial, Chan Benson, old Uncle Tom Cobleigh and all, as the ancient song says. It occurred to me to wonder whether there was some baleful influence in the atmosphere of Haven IV, or maybe in whatever rays from its sun hit the surface, that was softening my brain.

Sure: my obvious candidate was Supernumerary Willis. For all I knew, he had the necessary motive; he certainly had the means, if anybody did, for lifting the non-Jewels from under the noses, if they had any, of the Tock guardians. But Willis was no more than a candidate: given the motive, any human being on Haven IV might conceivably have been elected. I had my own prejudices in favor of electing one of the Consulate people but they were prejudices, not theories, for God's sake, facts. Any human being . . .

The thing to do, then, was to shut up. Why give whoever was behind the hysteria on Haven IV any more warning than absolutely necessary?

We were rolling along in fine style, at the legal top speed, which seemed fast enough to be dizzying. I shut my eyes, since I wasn't being shot at or actively annoyed for the moment, and tried to see if I could come up with anything more—or, for that matter, any real objections to my shiny new notion.

Objections didn't appear. But one novelty did: given, again, the motive, it wasn't terribly likely that I was working against one human being: it was the sort of thing that almost always involves a group, large or small. And such groups do exist—they always have, even pre-Space when their only targets were different-type groups of human beings—and, apparently, they always will.

I thought of a folk tale old enough to have cobwebs festooned all over its cobwebs: The Little Tailor. Remember? *Seven At One Blow*. I'd just wrapped and bundled five, which was a fair display that left me breathing heavily but otherwise unharmed; now—if, as I say, I had hold of the right motive—I was probably going up against a group of anywhere from ten to about eighty. The human colony on Haven IV was small, and that limited possible group size: much larger, and everybody would know the group existed. And that, I was sure, wasn't the case. Chan Benson, for instance, was a theoretical candidate—but in Benson's case it was a damned thin theory. Somehow, I doubted that he was the finest actor I had ever come across, professional or amateur; and, if he weren't, he didn't know about the group, and he didn't belong to it.

But I couldn't take the chance. Even though I knew perfectly well that the group I was thinking over might be a figment of my own bouncy imagination, working overtime just to give me some solid ground, after my visit to London.

I asked myself one more question: Was Willis a member of the group?

That one I thought I could answer. Almost certainly: he had to be, if there were a group at all. He was the wrong man, in the wrong place, with exactly the wrong equipment.

If, of course, there really were a group. . . .

I didn't doubt it for a second. Not, at least, after I heard the mob.

At first, I thought we'd come round in a circle or something, and were heading back into the scene of recent battle. But there were no sirens, and noise was unrestrained—which wouldn't be the case if the people behind the sirens had arrived. Those wide-focus freeze guns the cops like to carry, on most worlds, are the Hell of an effective argument.

So I opened my eyes. At the same instant, my driver said: "Sir?"

Sight restored, along with hearing, I didn't need any amplification from him. We hadn't circled back: he'd done his job with the expected efficiency, and taken me back to the Embassy. In front of which a middle-sized riot seemed to be taking place.

I said: "Drive on," and added at once: "But not far. Take us on past the garage, roll a few yards, and stop. I think I'm going to have to get involved again."

"Yes, Sir." He didn't sound doubtful or worried. Either he'd seen and appreciated my small performance—*Five At One Blow*—or he figured that I had to follow somebody's orders and report to the Embassy, and if that required fighting my way in then I was committed to fighting my way in. I don't know which, and didn't ask. The car, or tank, went right on past the riot— which seemed to be confined to the front door and perhaps eight feet in either direction down the sidewalk—past the garage, and rolled to a smooth stop against the sidewalk just three yards away. The rioters hadn't appeared to notice me—though I knew perfectly well that was somebody's clever idea: I had to be noticed, if only as an unidentified military vehicle coming up and stopping nearby, and most probably as Gerald Knave.

I took a good long look out the rear window, wriggling round in my seat to get the best view:

it was the only chance I was going to have to see the damned riot calmly. I wondered who, if anybody, had been killed. And the whole parade of killings rose up and began to bother me.

It's one thing to die because you are who you are, or dispose of the power or position you happen to dispose of. It's quite another thing to be killed because you happen to be there, and somebody has to be elected. All the deaths, except one, were like the first one I'd seen, Pollorine's—pure accident. I don't know why that feels worse than calculated murder, but it does. The exception—General Tal, of course—counted for something, but not enough: the scheme I had constructed, from everything I'd seen or been told, made me feel a little sick.

The riot, oddly enough, made me feel just a bit better. It was, for one thing, such an exceptionally stupid scene.

This time, there wasn't a lot of destruction. Embassies tend to be constructed along the lines of ancient Egyptian tombs (and so do Consulates—and so do most government buildings: the clear inference isn't worth drawing, not just now, but you can provide your own sketch of it), and they have weight and solidity on their side. A window or two might have been broken by somebody's rock, or thrown beamer, or slug, or perhaps even large shoe, but that would be about it. But the noise level was even higher, mostly because of the chants—and then there were the signs.

Posters, I suppose you might call them. The mob in front of the Embassy—thirty to forty people, some of them undoubtedly just come from the Tock restaurant before the freeze guns came into play—was fully supplied with the things. Large, on sticks, and dripping with messages. Like this:

HUMANS AND SNAKES
DON'T MIX

WIPE OUT ENEMY ALIENS
MAKE OUR WORLD
SAFE FOR HUMANITY

DO IT TO THEM
BEFORE THEY
DO IT TO HUMANITY

TOCKS DON'T
TICK RIGHT

I rather liked the last one. But the whole aggregation made no more sense than the sort of thing I'd had from the restaurant mob—which fit, of course. Making sense was going to be beyond this group—not the mob, but the human beings who had whipped up the mob. That didn't mean they were stupid, though it meant that the signs and slogans were pretty well guaranteed to be; but the sort of motive I was looking at never does make any noticeable sense.

This has never stopped human beings from getting involved with it. A last thought occurred to me as I got ready to open the right-hand door, nearest the sidewalk:

What was there to bother me about my being unable to explain the Tocks? I couldn't explain human beings, either; all I could do was to note that given activities didn't start from, or lead to, anything sensible. Which was a fair description of Tock society—wasn't it?

Well, no: what had bothered me most about the Tocks was that I couldn't tell which parts made sense, and which parts didn't. Apparently, I was perfectly comfortable pigeonholing scattered actions and motives as nonsense—*i.e.*, inexplicable—but a long way from comfortable once deprived of my pigeonholes.

So: every day we learn something new about ourselves. This is the single least cheerful fact I can think of. I sighed a little, and took a deep breath, and opened the door. The noise hit me full in the face as I turned.

Some of them were just screaming, and some were babbling. But most of the mob, that time, was chanting: more slogans, equally silly. I hadn't been able to distinguish words from inside the car, and I couldn't do much better outside it; only scattered bits came through the general whoopee. There was something about *Beat back the aliens,* and something else about *Monsters trying to kill humankind,* and a ragged chant that seemed to come back, over and over, to: *Humanity's living space requires Tock extermination,* which sounded awfully fancy as language for a chant, but who was I to criticize? Me, I hadn't chanted any slogans in years; maybe polysyllables were a new fashion, or the Coming Thing.

No Things, as it happened, were Coming at me: the mob, in fact, looked wonderfully orderly, in a scruffy sort of way. It was making its presence felt, and it was sure as Hell making its protest and its point of view known, but it wasn't doing anything else.

Why not?

The unassailable Embassy building wasn't enough reason: human beings don't make sense even one at a time, not really, and when you get a mob of them together sense is an item everybody has forgotten how to manufacture. No: they were marching and shouting, and nothing more, for a reason. It struck me that the reason was going to be important.

Who'd told them to do that? in other words. Somebody had orchestrated the scene, and I wanted to know his name, or hers. Even more badly, I wanted to know why.

That was the one thing I could depend on making sense: for all the scattering of bombs, and assorted deaths, and the one enormous theft, there was going to be a reason. A sensible reason—as far as anything that involves exploding bombs is sensible, and sometimes it is. I knew that much: I could feel it in my bones, as they say.

I could feel the damned mob in my bones, too, as I walked toward the Embassy front door. The shouting was as loud as possible, and the scruffy marching and waving of signs made walking a good deal trickier than usual: I had to pick my way up to the mob, through it (bumping into an occasional screamer, or waver, on the way), and straight on to the doors. When I was standing in front of them, the mob began to change shape, and a ragged semicircle of human beings, all of them silent, all of them waiting, surrounded me. If the doors opened, they were all set to join me, and they had a good spot for it—straining at the leash and all ready to crash the joint just as soon as I got the doors open for them. Could be they were just ambitious to do their chanting inside the Embassy instead of out on the sidewalk; but despite the weird peacefulness of the whole affair I kept remembering the various bombs.

, So I reached the doors, turned with my back against them, and pulled out two guns. For maybe half a second I must have looked like a 3V hero type—all I needed was a semi-naked gal draped fetchingly in the background, and somehow I didn't think Betty Gorgial would fill the role at all well.

The little half-circle around me looked with respect and interest at my guns. They got even quieter. Maybe half a minute passed while they went on inventorying the guns, and me, and now and then each other: their conversation was carried on in eyeblinks, shrugs, facial gestures and so on—about every wordless communication method there is, with your clothes on.

Then the circle faded back, away from me and the doors, and melted into the general mob. Which had been marching and waving its signs and chanting all this time, and which went right on doing that.

I reached over my shoulder and banged on one of the twin doors with the butt of my beamer. In about twenty seconds the door opened and I backed right on inside; two Robbies had let me in, and until they'd shut the doors behind me I didn't turn away from the mob on the sidewalk.

In the big lobby, there was a great deal of chatter. I tried not to listen to it for a bit: the scene that had just been played out for me, in front of the building, had been as weird as anything the Tocks had come up with: it made no sense at all.

And that, I knew perfectly well, was wrong. When I had things figured out, the peaceful mob would make sense: it had to.

But not until then.

CHAPTER NINETEEN

Trouble.

You might as well let that stand as a one-word description of the rest of that damned day.

If you want a slight expansion, here it is. If you want a full blow-by-blow, the Hell with the idea: I went through it all once, and I don't have to report it and go through it again that way. But the slight expansion:

Betty Gorgial lit into me as soon as I'd turned away from the shut doors. What had I done? and What was going on? and Did I realize that the situation was serious? and more silly questions than you could shake a Tock at, not to mention various expressions of panic and determination, most of them revolving around the idea that she had to get back to the Consulate, phone contact not being sufficient, and that the Consulate people were starting to go to pieces. What they needed, she kept saying, was a firm hand. She didn't tell me whose, and didn't have to, and wasn't asked. But shutting her up took a great deal of otherwise valuable time.

What I wanted was a small, enclosed spot in which I could sit and think for a while, far from the maddening God damned crowd. What I got was an avalanche: a little of everything, adding up to the Hell of a large load. Chan Benson had been thinking about the military revolt, and had come to the decision that only a Consulate man could assume power and hold it, which was sensible if not quite true, and he had a list of possibles (not including Supernumerary Willis—or General Roven, for that matter) he wanted to discuss, with full attention to their strong and weak points.

He still looked like somebody's nice uncle, and he was still, in a quiet voice and with as much calm as possible, making passable sense; but even Chan Benson was a bother.

I met a small collection of staff people, all of whom wanted to know what was going on, and when I was going to have it all straightened out. For the record:

1. Daniel Poss, First Undersecretary for Alien Affairs: short, undernourished, white-haired and almost completely covered with red tape, a good deal of which he tried to paste onto me.

2. Frederika v. Dinistan, Military Liaison Officer between the Haven II Embassy and the local armed forces—a job I didn't envy her. Dumpy, moon-faced, and a terrible tendency to try looking stern. She wasn't built for looking stern. She wanted to discuss the Army succession, too, but her ideas weren't even as sensible as Chan Benson's. Specialists tend to get lost in their specialties, and this one was stuck with the notion that the main purpose of the armed forces on Haven IV was to maintain good relations with the Embassy. She didn't say

"maintain good relations," naturally. What she wanted them to do was to "liaise satisfactorily." I pushed her off on Benson after a few minutes—well, half an hour: she was a persistent sort—and told her to compare lists with him. I did have a pang of sympathy for Benson, but if I were ever going to do the job I was being hired for I was going to have to get a great many people out of my hair.

3. Stane Lennine, and the trouble with things as they are is that, as soon as you get rid of Frederika v. Dinistan, somebody like Stane Lennine pops up. Communications Chief for the Embassy—IntraAmbassadorial Structures and Linkages. That translates into the guy who keeps the local phone circuits working. Of course the lobby bomb, a while back, had blown a noticeable portion of his network into impalpable dust, and of course what he wanted to know was whether I wanted the network repaired. I said Sure, if he could manage it without being underfoot all over the place, and he asked whether I was certain. I said Sure, and he wanted to know whether I'd considered all the factors. He had a large bundle of factors, which he wanted to show me bit by lovely bit. I said that a working communications net would be a thing of beauty and a joy forever. Give a good technician a large title, and once in a while he turns into Stane Lennine on you.

4.—and 5., and 6., and so on into the night. The lobby was crowded, partly because Benson and Gorgial had stayed there right through, as instructed, and the few people who didn't want to see Chan Benson wanted word on the Consulate from Betty Gorgial. Partly that, and partly the mob outside: there were nicely protected windows (vulnerable to a wide range of things, but with protective fields good for small items or low speeds), and lots of the Embassy staff had never seen a mob before. Lots of them had never seen me before, either, and it seemed I was a fair tourist draw.

The place was also crowded with people who'd heard about the mobs and about General Tal, and probably about the local bombs, and had come to the Embassy as the safest place they could think of, for God's sake, in which to wait things out, and ask questions.

(I assumed that the Consulate was not drawing a proportionately equal number of its own people—Haven III types. If the assumption turned out to be wrong, I had a horrible feeling I was going to have to go back to the drawing-board. And *that* was impossible: I had most of an explanation for why things had been happening the way they had, and the explanation was so entirely weird that there couldn't possibly be two of them. The assortment of events looked so very random—and was, in a way—that only one answer was going to get all of those events under the same roof.)

I fought my way through hordes of questions with people attached to them—it gave me a feel for the way a 3V star must have to live, which is not a recommendation for the experience—and found Chan Benson near the back of the lobby, still cornered by that gal with the passionate wish to get some liaising done.

She was saying: "But it is obviously important that members of each specific grouping be dealt with by other group members—" and I tapped nice Uncle Chan on the shoulder from behind.

"Sorry," I said. "I've got to have some information right away. Vital. From Mr. Benson."

Frederika v. Dinistan, dumpy, moon-faced, and nowhere near out of breath—she'd only had twenty minutes or so with Benson, between the time I'd pushed her off and the time I'd managed to fight my own way to the rear echelon—gave me a glare. "Surely someone else—" she began.

"I'm afraid not," I said, and looked firm and decisive. We were over near the left-hand glassex doors that led from the lobby into the cheery maze of the Embassy proper, where I'd been, it seemed, about three years before; I drew Benson toward them, holding onto his shoulder. He made some sort of placative motion at the v. Dinistan type with his hands, and turned to go with me. The expression on his face was positively plaintive with relief.

I tried to push open a door with my shoulder before I remembered that the things slid. Benson said: "Here. Let me—" and grabbed part of the running vertical handle just as I grabbed another part, a bit higher. We started to slide the door open, and something went *crash* and *tinkle,* and, God damn it, there went my plans for a quiet few minutes.

I didn't need to look: the sound had come from one of those front windows, back at the other end of the lobby. I made myself a private bet —one hundred to one or better—that whatever had come through had not come from the mob full of signs and chants. My best guess was a moving car, rolling very slowly or stopped just long enough to get a shot out through an open side window.

But my guesses could wait, and the situation couldn't. I didn't hear any hiss, tick or hum, not over the shouts and shrieks and general chatter of the entire lobby population, but I didn't need to. "Whatever had come through," I told myself —another little private bet: if I could figure out a way to pay myself off I think I could almost live on the earnings, some days—had come from a grenade launcher, and was, therefore—

Sure. I took a very short breath, having spent maybe fifteen seconds since the thing had arrived, and shouted, over all the madness, the hardest order I'd had to give since arrival.

"Follow me!"

Benson and I went through the doors. What seemed like one million lobby inhabitants came boiling through right behind us. One in a thousand, roughly speaking, was bright enough to head for the right-hand set of doors—they led to the same place, after all—but only one in a thousand.

I said: "Follow me," and they were, by God, going to follow me. Whether it made sense or not.

I was the guy who was going to straighten everything out, wasn't I? I was the guy who knew what he was doing, right?

So, the left-hand door. Moving fast, I leaned down a little and said: "Stairs?" and Benson nodded.

I yelled at the damned crowd: "Basement—down—", and apparently enough of them heard me to start a movement toward elevators, a sort of escalator-slidewalk, and even some sensible stairs, all heading into the bowels of the building.

One minute had passed. One minute and fifteen seconds.

What the Hell was it waiting for?

I said to Benson: "Up," and he nodded again, and we snaked around a staircase down which hordes were pouring, or whatever it is hordes do, came to a matching stair leading up, which was quite empty, and got nearly ten steps toward the second floor.

At which point—at last—the lobby blew up.

I hoped to Hell that the phone man had fixed enough of the system so I could get one call out. Chan Benson had stopped at the sound of the explosion, which was really one of your major sounds—it had been the Hell of a large lobby, and apparently it had been a powerful grenade —and I pulled him on to step eleven, and right on to the end of the flight without a pause.

God damn it—as usual, there just wasn't any time.

CHAPTER TWENTY

"My office?" Benson asked politely, once we were off the stairs, and into the second floor corridors.

"Sure," I said. The place looked and sounded weirdly peaceful (if you ignored the cries of panic and stampede coming from away down below, and I was glad to be able to): the floor was deserted. Corridors ran on, doors were shut or half open or open wide; and nobody was in the rooms, and nobody came down the corridors with a stack of flimsies, or official stats, or one of the Tock chair arrangements. Nobody came down the corridors at all. We were all alone.

Peace, it's wonderful. Turn right, travel the equivalent of five squares—a quarter-mile—turn right again, then left, straight, and just a touch more left, and we stopped in front of an opaqued door that looked like all the other opaqued doors. This one happened to be shut: Benson, his secretary-if-any, or both had a nice wide streak of neatness. I'm a housekeeping buff—I let my Totum and two Robbies clean the place, the dishes or the silver only when I feel depressed, or when I'm away, as on Haven IV— and, as such, I approve of streaks of neatness.

Benson opened the door and gestured me inside. For about one second I hesitated.

Well, damn it, it was still possible for my nice Uncle Chan to be a member of my hypothetical group. Just barely, but—

He noticed the hesitation, and smiled. He started to move in ahead of me, and I reacted to the smile—damn it, apparently the periodic concussion of all those explosions, plus the disoriented feeling I'd been carrying around since London, had done something serious to my brain—and moved, and we did a small Alphonse-and-Gaston ballet before he stepped back and let me go first.

Sure. Call Uncle Chan a member of the group. Say he had a fine, lethal surprise waiting for me inside his office.

Why wait for the office? We'd had a full staircase, and a complete set of corridors. If there was anything lethal in his plans, *in re* Gerald Knave, he'd had all the time in the world to try it, and he'd have had the weapons, too—whatever equipment he thought he needed. He had to know I was coming back, and, without knowing when, he had to be prepared.

I spell it out for you, in all of its obvious glory, because I had to see Benson's smile and then spell it all out for myself. By the time Benson was seated behind his desk—normal bureaucratic desk and chair set, with a neat stack of papers in an In basket and a slightly more ragged set in an Out basket, two telephones (green, with gold trim around the visual setup, and red, with black trim: a little gaudy for a bureaucrat, I thought, but maybe there was a secret itch for display under all that quiet sense-making), and a full scriber set. No pictures of the wife and kiddies, no holograms thereof, nothing else, and maybe he was calm because he was single, or single because he was calm—at any rate, by the time he got behind the desk and sat down, and I found a visitor's chair and dropped into it, the shrieking of the damned, or whatever the Hell it was, was nearly inaudible even if I tried to hear it. I didn't try.

The shrieking in my own head was noise enough.

Benson, looking perfectly at home—the explosion had stopped him, but not for long—said: "Well, Knave?"

"Phones," I said. "I have to find some time to think—but the first thing I need is a phone line. Outside."

Benson looked at his two doubtfully. "I have no idea," he said. "I've been in the lobby all this while: just what service has been restored I am not sure." He picked up the red phone first, punched out what was obviously an outside-call key number, and watched as the visual didn't light up. He tried it again, got nothing again, and moved over to the green phone with gold trim.

That one lit up. "Major outside communications seem to be operating," he said. "The other phone is keyed for exterior and interior calls; this is exterior only."

True: he hadn't bothered to punch a code. He'd just picked up the phone and punched Go.

I said: "Can we get London?"

"London?" He stared at me. For some reason a call to the Tocks didn't seem obvious.

"I've got to check something," I said. "And I want to know if there have been any disturbances out there. Of any kind."

"Well," Benson said, "the Jewels—"

"I mean now," I said. "Don't bother about the Jewels: we'll have those. But I'd like to have a functioning King and Queen to hand them over to."

Haven's sun had set, some while back. It had been a long day, and it seemed to be getting longer all the time. But the once-in-nine-days Tock chaos was coming along fast, and that was one thing I didn't want to have added to the rest of the mix. "Naturally," Benson was saying. "But do you really think there might be danger—"

"God damn it, man, give me the thing!" Impatience is a terrible vice; it was the one and only time I was ever sharp with my kind, sensible uncle. But the clock in my head kept ticking. Tocking? At any rate, we'd had killings, a theft, and now a truly massive bomb; God alone knew what the next stage was going to be.

God, and my hypothetical group, I supposed. Benson, looking positively shocked—defined as raised eyebrows, pursed lips, and a general air of drawing away from me about eighteen inches—cradled the phone, gestured at it gracefully, host to guest, and said: "Certainly. I'm sorry if I—"

"Sure you are," I said. "And so am I. It's just that we're working against time."

"But if you know about the Jewels—"

"The Jewels aren't the problem," I said. "They're part of the solution." Benson blinked at me, and I reached for the green phone and turned it so the visual display faced me and I could use the thing—I'd hitched my chair up to a corner of the desk—and picked up the receiver.

I almost punched Go. I stopped just in time, and asked Benson, in my most apologetic voice: "What's the number for London?"

"The Royal Palace private line? Of course . . . one moment," he said. He pulled open a drawer —a real, old-fashioned drawer, not a display console—and fished around in it, and came up with a small, limp book. He flipped through the pages while I waited. Impatience is a terrible vice, and patience is a virtue: I don't think I ground my teeth too much, or too audibly, while I waited. After five or six years—well, five or six seconds, anyhow—he looked up, calm as ever, and gave me a number.

I punched Go: the screen lit up: I punched in the number.

Surprise: on Haven IV we didn't have rings, and we didn't have blats. We had gongs, as if somebody were tolling a funeral service for the phones over the phone wires. Maybe they were: I didn't ask if the gongs were normal. I counted three and a half of them before the visual went into spots and dots, the way it does, and read-justed to show me a male Tock, standing more or less upright, holding a small Tock version of my receiver to his ear with a few front legs, or arms. Or whatever you want to call them: I've never come up with anything that satisfies me.

He said: "Who is calling? Please activate your pickup." Better pronunciation than most human beings, but phone people are like that.

I punched in the visuals at my end. "This is very important—" I started.

"Ah," the Tock said. "The human Knave. I have not seen you until now, but I have wished to: I can tell my aunts and nieces of this encounter. I am very glad to have been on duty when you called."

Fame, it's wonderful. If a reputation among Tock aunts and nieces was what you'd call fame. "Important," I said again. "I have to talk to His Majesty."

"His—ah," the phone Tock said. "Our Worshipful. Your slang is sometimes difficult." I had never thought of "His Majesty" as slang before. Nor since, for that matter. "But I am afraid that conversation, at this moment, is beyond possibility."

"Now, look—" I started.

"I am doing so," the Tock said. "Indeed, I should like to look my fill, and appreciate your condescension toward one of my major senses. My gratitude, as I have said or implied—"

Impatience is not only a terrible vice, it's hard on the teeth. I was grinding away as if the practice were my newest career. "Never mind gratitude," I said. "I told you: important. Knave. I don't care what he's doing—if you give him that message he'll be right on the line here."

"Undoubtedly he would be," the Tock said. "But it is impossible to do so: Our Worshipful

felt the need for contemplation and understanding, and he has therefore gone to the Great
Hall to disembody himself for a period. In a few
hours, perhaps—"

Disembody himself for a few hours? I felt that
uneasy sensation creep into my bones again, as I
was faced with something I couldn't understand
and couldn't file. Maybe disembodiment would
help understanding. If it helped Nassanank. . . .

I grabbed hold of my own mind before it
began going in circles tight enough to bite its
own damned tail. "Can't you—well, bring him
back?"

"Back?" the Tock said. "He has never left.
But disembodiment, especially in the Great
Hall, is under the control of Our Worshipful
Himself, and none other."

"A few hours may be too late!" I said.

The Tock regarded me with what, when I recall it and match it against Tock expressions I've
begun to know, looked a lot like patient sympathy. It is an odd expression on the face of a semi-
snake. "Is it necessary that you talk only with
Our Worship Himself?"

"Oh," I said. "Sure. Of course it isn't. Unless
your Queen—whatever her title is—"

"She is not our Queen. She is, officially, Egg-
Warmer and Main Twiner to Our Worshipful.
She is addressed as Our Wondrous—a weak
translation into your speech, but the best we
have yet discovered. And she is, to the best of my
belief, available for conversation on this chain of
instruments."

"Fine," I said. Better, in a way: Nassanank

would have all the facts, and so would Jessiss, but Jessiss would be a lot faster with them. "Go and have her paged. Or whatever it is you do."

"Your wish is my delight," he said in a perfectly sober voice.

"Fine. Page her."

"I shall inform the mother of her Medium," he said. "Please wait: I am sure that Our Wondrous will be extremely happy to speak with you, and will be doing so soon—within a minute or less."

I let him go through the whole speech. If you interrupt one of those Standard Replies, all you do is make the guy start over again. When he was through I said: "Fine. Do that."

The mother of her Medium? A brainless creature, who had no direct dealings with the King and Queen, as far as anybody had been able to tell me. . . .

Confusion, as somebody has said, worse confounded. The Hell of a lot worse.

Night was coming. I was tired as all Hell; I took it as a fair assumption that my hypothetical group was tired, too, and that any more outbursts would wait until morning. But it was only an assumption: anything might happen, and anything might already have happened. Benson looked at me, his face unchanged, his head just beginning to nod. The visual had gone spots-and-dots again, and the system was playing music at me. A magnificent ancient: *Yesterdays*. Where had I been yesterday? I thought. And why hadn't I stayed there?

Benson's head was nodding, his body swaying

a bit in time to the music. The little man was half asleep: little man, you've had, I should think, at least as busy a day as I've had. And I don't think you're used to it.

The seconds went on going by, one at a time, on parade. I listened to *Yesterdays,* and tried to think of the group of musicians who'd written it (and finally came up with it, in case it's bothering you too: the Bottles), and began counting the spots-and-dots.

The Tock had been right: in just under a minute the music faded, the spots and dots dissolved, and I was looking at Jessiss.

"Well?" she said.

"Your Wondrous," I began, and she cut me off.

"Important," she said. "Urgent. Do you have time to play games with your vocabulary?"

Well, no. "All right," I said. "Questions. First: has there been any disturbance in or around London?"

She nodded and blinked both eyes. Decided agreement. "A group of humans has been chanting and parading with signs before our main entrance—on territory ceded for use by both races, so there is little we can do on our own, as you say."

I hadn't said a thing. "Chants and parades. That's it?" I asked.

"The signs are most offensive," she said. "Several Media and six of our young—including a grandmother-nephew!—have been greatly disturbed by them."

"All right," I said. "Do what you can for them

—prevent others from seeing the signs or hearing the chants. They're going on here, too."

Jessiss looked surprised. "Chants against our people? In purely human territory?"

I don't know how she had it taped that I was calling from purely human territory like the Embassy, and not mixed-race territory, like the street where the restaurant had been. Maybe her phone link had an automatic ID built into it for incomings. Maybe she recognized the background. "Chants of all sorts," I said. "But has there been anything else?"

"Ah," she said. "The gross disturbances of which you told us. I am afraid not: gross disturbances might be dealt with, but simple chanting and the carrying of large posters does not lend itself to easy treatment. I shall keep your suggestion in mind, as regards such matters. But nothing else has occurred here; I am quite sure of that."

"You've been in your body all the time?" I said. "Not disembodied like Nassanank?"

Jessiss stared at me. "As it happens, I have," she said. "I have been allowing several suitors to polish my carapace; the Royal Habit of so doing has a calming effect on our people. But what does disembodiment have to do with your question?"

I was damned if I knew. I told myself, in a soothing manner, that maybe we had a language barrier. I didn't believe that for a second.

"All right, then," I said. "No violent disturbances. Any signs of violence building up— violence against London?"

"No signs whatever," she said.

I nodded. "Fine," I said. "It simplifies things."

"On the contrary, it complicates them," she told me with what I can only call asperity.

"From my point of view—"

"You must not allow yourself to be carried away by your own point of view," she said, very earnestly. "Accede to the world-view of others, even strangers; thus their being is added to yours, and yours to theirs."

"Sure," I said. For once, Jessiss sounded like one of the nut religions that keep cropping up. Thus the aura of your reincarnated Being (always in caps) is added to the aura of Being itself, and is permitted to turn to the Supernal Shade of Purple. But, in Jessiss' terms, maybe it made sense. They were Tocks, not humans.

It occurred to me to wonder, briefly, whether the human colony on Haven IV was still entirely human—or was beginning to borrow, here and there, from the Tocks. Give the place a hundred years, and it might not be recognizable to Tock or human being; people who deal with each other all the time tend to share views, and swap standpoints.

But that had nothing to do with the subject. "Never mind the point of view," I said. "Outside London—would you know—have there been any Tock casualties? Or any human casualties that the Tocks were involved in?"

"I would know, with certainty," she said. "A few bruises, such as the ones our fellow beings received in the restaurant battle you involved yourself in. No more, on either side. And may I thank you for your defense of our people. They are, of course, not sane, and so not fully able to defend themselves—"

"Not sane?"

"No Tock who makes a trade of dealing with human beings can be thought of as entirely sane," she told me.

Well, all right.

And I had my answers. "Good. Fine. Just stay where you are—inside London—bring as many of your people back to London as you can—and you'll be safe."

"And the—the—theft?" She whispered it as if it were an obscene word. Maybe it was; maybe it is.

"That will straighten out, too," I said. At any rate, the odds were with me. "Before you leave the Throne, I believe."

"In two more days?"

"Or less," I said. "Depending. Thanks: I'm cutting off now."

"Respect and good feeling to you," she said, and blanked out. I punched Stop and the visual went dark.

Benson was blinking with weariness, but looking at me. I gave him my very best nod. "It's going to be all right," I said. "Nothing should happen until morning. Let's all get some sleep, for God's sake."

CHAPTER TWENTY-ONE

And we actually did. Benson was better than half-asleep right there in his office, and I tiptoed out and shut the door and left him there, the door being self-locking. I took one deep breath and headed on down to the basement via stairway and told everyone to try to rest, they were perfectly safe. I think I even believed it. They wanted a great deal more, of course, but I was not providing any more; after a while I managed to fight my way free, come back to Benson's deserted floor, and find the office next to his. I suppose there were beds somewhere, but I didn't want to ask anybody—Hell, I didn't even want to *see* anybody—so I lay down on an inoffensive light blue rug and shut my eyes. Was the door closed? I opened my eyes. Locked? Once more. No other door or window passage; the walls were thin, but I thought I could live with that. I put my ears on high gain, full alert, and my eyes shut again and I was gone.

Dreamland. They do say that if you sleep on a problem the answer will be revealed to you when you wake up. They say even sillier things, but that one does seem to work once in a while. Not very often. And I had two problems. In order of increasing difficulty:

1. Who? Mostly, Why gives you Who. Sometimes it doesn't, and that was one of the some-timeses. Proper consideration called for Holmes and his LSD beaker, plus a computer run on every human inhabitant of the planet. One small logical hole hit me, and I filed it to patch in the morning; but I didn't have time for proper procedure, and beakers of LSD were unavailable. A good thing, too: I'll think about experimenting with new realities when I've exhausted the possibilities of this one, but that hasn't happened yet.

2., and the real toughie: So what do I do? Knowing the answer was not going to be enough. Telling everybody the answer was not going to be enough—for one thing, the population had been carefully rigged, with, probably, fair success, not to believe it. I might even get the non-Jewels back, and still be stuck with a mess: sure, that recovery was what I'd been hired for, but leaving things in the bloody chaos they were milling around in didn't seem like the thing to do, recovery or non-recovery. I was a Survivor, wasn't I? And if the Tocks were going to survive, I had to come up with something to do. Hell, if the human settlement were going to survive . . . or maybe all the Haven settlements (what the Tocks were capable of, I have never been quite sure) . . .

If you sleep on a problem the answer will be revealed to you. I slept, and when I woke up what had been revealed to me was that Betty Gorgial was really a Saurian from Rasmussen, and all the Tocks had gathered in their Great Hall to sing *Yesterdays,* in lovely harmony. Somehow, this did not seem helpful. I brushed the remains of the dream out of my head, and stood up and fished through pockets for a comb and a static toothbrush (my shaver was with my baggage, and my baggage was either still in the Embarcation Building or tucked away in an Embassy hidey-hole—unless, of course, it had been blown up by one or another of the recent explosions). I greeted the beautiful morn, as the poet says, and if you don't mind let's leave it right there, all right? A while later I was more or less human again, though wrinkled and a little scratchy around the face.

Chan Benson, I told myself, was still sleeping. I'd heard no sound. My ears, on alert all night, hadn't notified me of anything. The walls were thin.

But I still didn't hear any sound. I grabbed my door open, went four steps down to his, rattled the knob and banged on the thing. Then I waited.

Then I did some more rattling and banging.

I was fully prepared to beam my way in and discover the body when a weary, distant voice said: "Yes? Yes?"

"Knave here," I said. "It's morning. I think we'd better get down to where the people are."

A long pause, and then: "Ah. Yes. One moment."

Apparently, Benson was in the habit of greeting the beautiful morn the way I did. Though maybe not: sleeping curled up in your own office chair can fray the most even of composures. I

said: "Fine: I'm next door," and went away. I
left my door open, but nothing happened until
he arrived, still blinking, and pushing his wispy
hair back into place with his fingers.

Whereupon, damn it, we headed downstairs.

I still had no answers to my two questions.
But, as usual on Haven IV, I just plain didn't
have the time to scrabble around and get any.
We were going to have to go with what I had. Or
less.

The basement, when we got to it, was something out of Dante's Hell. It was crowded with
moaning people, trying to stretch a bit and
bumping into each other, starting small arguments, all of the whole miserable crew looking
even worse than mornings usually feel. There
was light, from flickering recessed panels along
the ceiling-wall junctures. I stopped four steps
from the bottom of the stairway, Chan Benson
behind me another three good steps or better,
and surveyed the big room. It had some long
tables and a few chairs, now pushed crazily into
positions that didn't mean anything; the ceiling
had a small array of piping shooting along it,
curving here and making ninety-degree turns
there and connecting with itself whenever it felt
the need. Nobody noticed me for the first few
seconds, while I was making this inventory.

Then I said: "Now hear this!" and the moaning and bumping subsided. It didn't stop; there
were just too many people in too small a space
for that. But a lot of the inhabitants of that un-
derground Hell did shut up, and turn round,

and stare over at me.

Chan Benson, behind me, said: "Knave is here by my orders. You will follow him as you would me." Or something like that; his voice was weak, against the remaining sounds, and he more or less trailed off when he realized that he was too high to be seen, and that nobody was even trying to see him. What eyes had managed to focus were focussed on me.

"I want two groups," I said. "Those with ties to Haven III—born there, or hired by the Consulate, or whatever—over near the front of the basement—" which was to my left "—and those with ties to Haven II and its Embassy over by the back. I want as much separation of groups as I can get."

Murmurs. "But we're here," a voice called. "On Haven IV."

Well, yes: people do go on telling you things you already know. I have no idea why: maybe they think it's helpful.

On the other hand, maybe they just don't think. It sounds, I'm afraid, like a much more reasonable hypothesis.

"The ones who aren't sure whether they're hired by Haven II or Haven III—shopkeepers, a few technicians, anyone else—form a group at the side of the room, the far side—" which was straight ahead of me. "And try to make it a small group. I know there are people here whose loyalties are basically to Haven IV, but I'd like them to think those loyalties over, and try to decide whether Haven IV would be better served by Haven II or Haven III. If you can make that decision, join the appropriate group; if you can't, join the Undecideds against the far wall. Ten minutes."

It took more like thirty, of course, all of it technicolor mania—but if I'd said thirty I'd have had seventy. Chan Benson said to me, in a voice meant to carry nowhere past the stairway: "What will this accomplish?"

"Chan," I said, "I am not entirely sure. But I think—I think, or maybe I just hope—that if I can get these people properly into bunches I may stop a war."

"A—"

"War," I said. "Horgai Tal would have been good at that: some special Generals are. That's part of why he was killed. He might have stopped the war—and there are people who don't want it stopped."

Chan Benson made a sound like *hmmm,* and stayed quiet for a minute. Then he said: "I see. Of course. And the Jewels—"

"Exactly," I said. "The only remaining question is: Who?"

"But that, surely, is obvious," he said. "What will be needed is a means of dealing with the situation: a person who can replace Tal as effective head of the Haven IV colony—someone calm, sane, trustworthy, reasonably intelligent—"

"Right," I said. I had that candidate in mind; the least of my troubles. And selling him to the populace at large didn't seem like a terribly difficult job. But my candidate wasn't going to be a full solution: the whole damned structure had to be broken down. . . .

While I was thinking this, I was noticing one of the inhabitants of Dante's Hell working her way through the shifting masses of unhappy people straight toward me. No surprise: I accepted my fate, and greeted the Gorgial as politely as possible.

She came to the staircase and leaned against her side of the open-work balustrade, looking up at me. If the balustrade hadn't been there, I could easily have kicked her wig off, if she wore a wig: she was just about that far below. I repressed the thought, not without a sense of loss.

"Well, Knave?" she said. "When will I be allowed to return to the Consulate? I am needed there. General Roven is attempting to establish relations with the Consulate, as ranking officer of the armed forces here; something will have to be done."

I was, at that moment, honestly curious. "What?" I asked her.

"He must be replaced," she said. "He has no conception of the proper role of the military in this situation. Perhaps this other man—what's his name?—"

"Willis," I said, and began to have a sinking feeling. She had no business forgetting that name, Dante's Hell or not. No business at all.

"Yes. Willis," she was saying. "Perhaps he could have managed matters satisfactorily as military commander; but we shall have to choose someone else, and have him publicly confirmed as soon as possible."

I wasn't really listening. "Have him publicly confirmed . . ." Well, for some reason, the vari-

ous Comity basic religions went through my
head. Willis, being confirmed and celebrating
his first communion. Willis, being confirmed—
bar mitzvah, they call it in that religion—and
beginning his traditional speech, the preSpace
version that makes sense only if you dig around
and do the Hell of a lot of research: "Today I am
a fountain pen." Willis being confirmed as a re-
sponsible subject of Allah—muezzin time, or
The Horn Blows at Midnight, as the preSpace
facsicles say. Willis. . . .

Ah, yes: Willis. I dragged my mind back from
its fresh fields and pastures new and pointed its
nose at the trail to hand, if that collection of
metaphor makes any sense.

Betty Gorgial was still talking, no surprise. I
broke in just as she was getting to: "A list of
acceptable, dependable candidates can be
drawn up in a few—"

"Right," I said, and meant every word. "Go
and draw it up. And bring it here as soon as
you're finished."

"May I ask what you intend to do with it?"
she said. A voice as cold as your toes in mid-
winter, and less active; a look in the eyes as
blank and all-knowing as if she were a Buddha,
contemplating its navel. Or novel. Or, I suppose,
navy, as part of the armed forces she needed a
commander for.

They wouldn't accept a female commander,
obviously: everything I'd seen and heard about
Haven III made that clear. The remaining
FemLib types, if they ever heard about Haven
III, might just come flying out to burn the place

down; it wasn't exactly your standard model sample for equality among human beings. (Though there was no objection to using any sex as cannon fodder: I'd seen that, along with General Roven, the day before—and seen it again in the restaurant riot.) So there had to be a male—which would make Gorgial the power behind that particular Throne—which would make . . .

Sure. "I intend," I said, sounding just as casual as if I were telling the truth, "to use it as a base list from which to choose the new commander."

She smiled at me. Not one of your nicer smiles: it looked as if it had been carved on her face, in a hurry, with a sharp knife. "Very well," she said. "I shall have the list at once."

I was quite sure she would, too—damn it.

Chan Benson, who had had the good sense to shut up during the exchange, said quietly: "Knave, surely you aren't going to—"

"I need that list," I said. "Give it a minute, and you'll see why."

It didn't take a minute. I watched people mill around down on the basement floor, and in less than forty seconds Benson's soft voice said: "Oh. Of course."

"Right," I said.

"But the Jewels—" he began.

Go ahead: the standard cartoon. A light panel went on over my head. I was agape. (Well, actually, I wasn't, and the light panel didn't suddenly kick in. But the cartoon picture fits.)

"The Jewels," I said. "Right. Now I know Who. I also know just how to handle this."

"But, Knave," Benson said. People were still milling around down there. A little shoving was going on.

"Fields?" I said.

"Protective sheets?"

"Right. Where, and can you go and get the things? I don't really trust anybody else: I haven't had time."

"Wait," he said, "I will return shortly." He turned and took two steps upward, and stopped. "Knave," he said, "are you sure that you know just how—I mean, it's a delicate matter. One false move—"

"So I won't make any false moves," I said. "My God, I haven't got that many moves to make. And if I can get those sheet fields, neither will anybody else. Right?"

"Ah—right," he said. He started on up the stairs again, and I mentioned that we were in a hurry, and he turned a fast climb into a positive zip.

The groups were beginning to form. The center of the room was just about empty: people wandered through it, heading for one group or another (and the Undecideds were shrinking as I watched, thank God: every few seconds one of them would peel off toward II or III). I had nothing to say, so I didn't say it.

I saw Betty Gorgial in a corner over on her side of the room, the Haven III side, with a pad and pencil—a real pencil, as far as I could tell at a distance: maybe the things were status symbols—making up her list.

Good. Fine. When Chan Benson, good old

Uncle Chan, returned with the flat generators for sheet fields . . .

But he wasn't going to return. Too much time had passed. He'd run into a group member, hiding in the destroyed lobby (the staircase was hidden from the lobby proper: I hadn't really taken a look at the mess, and decided it would be a good idea, when I had a few minutes), and the group member had beamed him into ash. He'd tripped and broken his fool, valuable neck. He'd switched on a field accidentally, and it had sliced him in two.

There are a lot of possible catastrophes. I went through quite a long list. The footsteps coming down the stairs, at last, were more of a relief than you can imagine.

"Wrong keys, wrong closet," he said. "I had to go to the Detention Equipment Room—not that we use it much, but Embassy rules require it—and locate the right key—"

"Tell me later," I said. He'd brought three generators: the Hell of a weight for a kindly old uncle. Above me by the same three steps, he was panting a little as he handed them on down.

I fixed them on the stairs above and below me, and the flat sheet right in front of me. I don't think Betty Gorgial noticed.

But somebody did. Before I could switch anything on, I felt a sudden rise in temperature right along my left ear.

CHAPTER TWENTY-TWO

A beamer, and a damned near miss. I had the generators on in one-tenth of a second—all right, call it one-fifth, but no more—and sent up a small prayer of thanks. Shooting up at an angle isn't very easy, and the group member hadn't had much time—but, even so, he'd come close. I was going to need burn treatment for that ear.

The left ear: sure. And, a second after the sheets went up, I saw a sparkle: a tight, hot beam wasting itself against a sheet field. It hadn't come from Betty Gorgial. There was a clump of people, and I couldn't locate my ambitious killer among them—not quite. I had the feeling that he was the weedy, untidy gent with the brown hair that stuck out all over his head like some ungodly nest. I wouldn't have sworn to it, and it didn't really make the Hell of a lot of difference. They don't make a lot of noise, and only a few people had seen the sparkle. I climbed up to the top of my voice and used it to cut through any remaining mumbles.

"You are all shielded," I told them. "This is the normal flat field: it passes voice, normal air mix and very slow, very small motion. Nothing else. You are all, now, safe."

Nobody said anything. Well, what did I expect? A rising vote of thanks?

"Each group is individually shielded. No chances will be taken. But I must confer with one person from the Haven III group. Will she come—slowly—through the field, with her list?"

There was some muttering and head-turning. Gorgial moved with all the assurance of a born leader, if you want a pretty picture, or with all the arrogance of a total egotist, if you don't. She hit the flat field, stopped, and moved as slowly as possible through it: six inches took her as many minutes. I waited: we all did. Every eye in the place was on her—even Benson's.

Once through, she walked straight on up to my post with no delay, and handed me a pad. There were five names on it.

I'd thought the group had been larger than that. But Gorgial, I supposed, knew better than I did: she was a part of it.

Even after the infighting—as I've said, Haven III was no different from most simple dictatorships, and there was a good deal of resentment about having a woman so high in the councils—that had very nearly got her killed, at least twice.

I didn't count the final lobby bomb. That had been display, pure and simple. Well: simple, at any rate. But Gorgial had been on the spot in the car, and she'd been on the spot when the reception desk went up. Either jobbie could have done for her.

Apparently, she bore no active resentment.

Powers behind Thrones often can't afford that particular luxury.

She stood on the basement floor, just below me, looking up at me half the time, and all around at Dante's (nicely grouped) Hell the other half of the time. I cleared my throat.

That was enough. The crowd acted as if I were going to announce either the end of the world, or else a six weeks' vacation with pay, away over on Apelles or, if possible, a better pleasure planet.

"Will the following persons please step forward?" I said, and read off the names on the Gorgial list. As expected, all were male; also as expected, all came from the Haven III end of the room.

As they were working their various ways through the crowd, and then the field, I said: "These men have been suggested as leaders of this colony, to replace General Tal." A general stir: the Hell of a lot of general stir, in fact. I ignored it. "I don't know them very well. I may want histories, accounts of character—"

"And who the Hell are you to ask for them?" A rough voice, and female: one of the Undecideds, I saw in a second, a good-looking gal if you like broad shoulders and great heft. Good for her.

"I'm Gerald Knave," I said. "Most of you have heard of me by now. I don't intend to make your final selection for you. But, if I have enough facts, I may be able to make a few suggestions. You'll be free to ignore them, if you like."

"Sure we will," the big gal said. Black medium-length straight hair, and she weighed more than I do at about the same height. Not the Hell of a lot more. In condition—for anything. If, as I say, you happened to like the type.

"You will," I said. "I have no way of enforcing them."

"These shields—"

"Very well," I said. "I'll release them, as soon as it can be done." I'd given Benson a sketch of the action while setting up the generators, and he went right to work. He began fiddling with the generator aimed at the Consulate group— fiddling as if it were hard and complicated work for him to turn the thing off. I made a show of bending down and asking him something, and he gave me an answer, and I told the crowd: "A small problem with the primary periodic beam. It shouldn't take more than a minute."

More stirring. Mumbling. It subsided, as everybody watched Benson work. A few people shouted suggestions, on the order of: "Try switching the X35 block with the 5N3s." Benson nodded to every one, and went on fiddling. He even managed to work up a convincing sweat.

The five on the list had joined Gorgial just under me. I needed at least one more, but he was going to have to wait: nothing in the scene would have fished him out. And the six I had were the group heads, at the least—the group heads or, minus one, the group.

I said: "All right, now," and Benson moved.

He switched off the generator covering the Embassy crowd—and instantly switched it on again, re-aimed and focussed (he was as good with standard field generators as most of us are; in sketching the scene, I'd checked that) to wrap my six little candidates in their own private field.

I said: "Haven II: you're unshielded. You can't be hurt: the other groups are behind shields, and the six here have a shield of their own they're stuck with." Lots and lots of mumbles and stirrings and murmurs.

Well, there was nothing to do but start explaining. At long last I was going to do my job: report to the Embassy and Consulate on the theft of the Crown non-Jewels.

Not to mention a good deal more.

I took a deep breath. Betty Gorgial was looking at me with an expression that was halfway past any ordinary glare, and halfway into the sort of frenzied insanity you hear about, and never actually see. She was actually trembling with the desire to get at me.

The five candidates didn't look any happier. Not that I expected them to.

"To begin with," I said, "the Crown Jewels of the Tock Monarchy are locked safely away—probably in the Consulate offices, but just possibly in a private home." Two of the candidates reacted with a sort of horrid surprise, and that pinned it down: the offices. A good deal safer, inside one of those Egyptian tomb buildings, than a private home was likely to be—if you didn't want the home to begin attracting undue attention.

The Embassy people were beginning to wander out onto the floor. The murmurs rose, and fell; there was some shoving and staggering, but not very much. When I cleared my throat again, I got instant silence.

"I think I'd better tell you what's been happening—because it hasn't been what you think it's been." One more deep breath, and I was launched. I hate long explanations.

CHAPTER TWENTY-THREE

Nassanank and Jessiss, oddly enough, needed a good deal less. Well, it takes non-humans to study human beings; and I suppose it helps to understand anything if you're the target of it.

It also helps, I think, if you happen to be Nassanank. Or—much superior—Jessiss.

"These human beings," she said, next day. "They would actually arrange for their own kind to die—die permanently, I mean—in order for this to happen?"

"As permanently as possible," I said. "There had to be a shock effect: that was what hit me when I really tried putting together all that had happened. Bombs, guns, even the theft—maximum shock. And riots—anti-Tock riots."

"But such riots were not generally dangerous," Nassanank said. "At least, our food technicians—thanks to your prompt action—were unharmed, and elsewhere there was very little danger to any Tock."

"Right," I said. "That was what got me: there should have been. There should have been the Hell of a lot more danger to everybody—angry mobs in front of the Embassy that really tried to do something, maybe using a beamer here and there on the doors or windows; attacks on all sorts of Tock establishments, involving the deaths of several Tocks—"

"This is scarcely possible," Jessiss murmured. Snakes, or at any rate Tocks, have an odd murmur—worth hearing, if you happen to be out toward the Haven system. "It cannot be imagined."

"It can by human beings," I said. "We do things like that; we're not Tocks. We cause deliberate damage; we kill. Or, at any rate, we ought to."

Nassanank said, with blank shock: "*Ought to?*"

"If the situation had been what it seemed to be, sure," I said. "I'm not recommending it as a normal course of conduct—maybe Tocks live better lives, though maybe not. I'm not an impartial judge. But the sheer lack of the sort of death and damage I've been talking about didn't make any sense. A few bombs, one solid revolution—against the new head of the armed forces, a man friendly to alien races and, of course, known to be so—"

"How known?" Nassanank said. Jessiss began a slow, impatient coil on her Throne—we were sitting around, drinking coffee, on my last day, and theirs: the next day, the Tock regulated chaos would reign.

"Willis," the Queen said. "I am sorry to interrupt, but surely it is clear that one member of a military establishment, especially a small one, would know such facts about another, highly placed member."

Nassanank blinked and nodded. I said: "Sure. So we had all that—and we had a total absence of what should have gone with it, in the normal —normal for human beings—course of events."

"Very well," Nassanank said. He sipped coffee and took a short puff on his water-pipe. That's another sight: a Tock with a water-pipe. Just a little like an octopus playing the bagpipes; but Nassanank thought of it as his one vice, and everyone was very indulgent about it.

"So, of course—" I started.

"But merely knowing that the course of events was senseless," Nassanank cut in, breathing out a little smoke, "could not have told you the true structure."

"The true inwardness," Jessiss said. She did have that habit: every so often she turned into a Mystic Religion on you for about eight words. I've put up with a good deal worse, from women I liked a good deal less.

"Yes," Nassanank said. "Many human events are, in fact, senseless: we have determined this."

Jessiss made an impatient move with her rear ten legs. Arms. At any rate, I forestalled any asperity among the upper classes by cutting in at once:

"But they're not senseless to human beings. There was a group of incidents; they had to be connected; and, if connected, they had to be planned. The planning mind didn't have to be sane, of course—"

"You see?" Nassanank cut in.

"—but it had to have reasons, reasons another human mind could dig out. Most human reasons for action may not be sane, from where you sit—or from where I sit, either—" Well, actually, I was in a sort of lotus position on a large cushion — "but they hang together. They make one structure. And as soon as I went looking for that one structure, I realized that I had to ask what the actions were supposed to accomplish."

Nassanank made a sound like a question mark. Jessiss said: "Yes. They appear to have accomplished nothing but chaos."

I nodded, and took another large ration of my own coffee. The Tocks serve better coffee than most people—or, at any rate, their Royalty does. "Chaos," I said. "All right: now suppose that chaos is what they were supposed to accomplish. A theft that had no other purpose—the Crown Jewels couldn't be sold anywhere, on or off the planet—bombs placed at random, killing human beings just because they happened to be around—"

"But your General Tal—a good human specimen; we shall be sorry for his loss, when our sorrowful period next occurs—was not killed by accident."

"Right," I told the King. "Like the revolt against General Roven, that was aimed at a high figure known to be friendly with Tocks. And he was more: he held the human colony here together. Once he was gone, no equal force remained; the colony could be swayed by nearly any emotion; it could be fragmented, and led."

Jessiss made a thoughtful sound. "I see," she said. "I think I see, at any rate: human beings are not easy to understand."

"No: not even for human beings," I told her. "No intelligent race is, or can be: there's too much free will in the mix." I waited for Nassanank to say: "Quite so," which he did, and went on. "Once I began to get the notion that chaos was the objective behind everything that was happening—a particular sort of chaos, at that—the rest fell into place."

"No," Nassanank said. "I do not see how this winds out of that."

"All right, look," I said. "Human beings were being mysteriously killed—by unknown devices that clearly weren't planted by other human beings, since they killed mostly at random, and they killed both Haven II and Haven III types. More Haven II, but that was an ignorable statistic, if you didn't know where a bomb might go off next. And if human beings weren't doing it—why, then, all the killing was the work of Tocks."

"But we *wouldn't*—" Jessiss said, absolutely horrified.

"Sure," I said. "I know that, and you know that. And everybody else knows it, and it's written about, and taught in the books. But nobody believes it. Deep down—and not so deep, at that—the idea of a non-violent, law-abiding race—law-abiding in our terms, I mean—is just too tough to swallow."

"Swallow?" Nassanank said, and then: "Ah. Idiom. I see." He took in some more smoke and dampness. "So it was possible for them to believe us—capable of such things. And what was done was done in order to create this belief?"

"Create it, or help it along," I said. "And re-move the people—General Tal, General Roven—who stood in the way of anything like normal Tock-human relations. All except for one thing: the Crown Jewels themselves."

"Yes," Jessiss said. "We are most grateful. Our curtains are yours."

I nodded and finished the coffee. Jessiss rang for a servant, and I went on: "The theft of the Jewels was aimed in the other direction. Max-imum friction: while the bombs, and then the staging of the riots—a few people who knew what was going on leading a great many people who never will, you might say—were meant to crank up human feeling against Tocks—you saw the signs, some of them, and I've told you some of the others—"

"Indeed," Nassanank said. "Most amusing."

"Not to human beings," I said. "Not under a growing strain. And—not altogether amusing even to Tocks. You told me of a few cases of dis-turbance—or, at any rate, Jessiss did. Humans were being led, very well and very fast, into hat-ing Tocks. And the theft—well, if you hadn't got the Jewels back, Tock feeling against human beings might have grown a little unpleasant."

This time it was Jessiss who said: "Indeed," Nassanank being preoccupied with his vice. A servant arrived and Jessiss took the tray and served more coffee round. When he had gone, she went on: "They wished us to dislike them?"

"They were looking for a war," I said. "Their notion was the notion on those signs: Tocks ought to be eliminated. Haven IV for human beings. It wasn't an idea they could have sold to the Comity—or to the Haven IV population, or the Haven II population either: I am just not sure about Haven III, straight, all by itself. But they wanted to force a Tock-human war, and wipe the Tocks off the planet. There's a lot of prejudice around, of all sorts—always has been, always will be—among human beings. And the notion that alien beings ought to be wiped out—kept in their place if possible, but otherwise disposed of—does keep cropping up. If they could create enough friction on both sides, they'd have their war."

Nassanank was going at the water-pipe as if his life depended on it. He was hearing ideas he had never imagined before—death, war, theft, hatred—and he needed time to regain his balance.

So did Jessiss—about thirty seconds. Then she said, very calmly: "And the human beings expected to win this war?"

I shrugged. "Of course they did. People like Willis—the one I couldn't round up in that basement, but easy enough to locate once I had the others, or most of the others—" There had been two more group leaders, not counting Willis, both at the Consulate. The Embassy doesn't maintain a large force on Haven IV, but it can get one when it wants it: those two, and Willis, had presented no difficulty. "People like Willis had developed techniques for blanking out the Tock mind—which is how the Jewels were stolen, as I mentioned—"

"Oh, yes," Jessiss said. "Those techniques.

And, doubtless, others—means to control our race physically."

I shrugged again, and drank some coffee. It was really remarkably good—not up to my own brew, but not at all despicable. "Well, sure," I siad. "I suppose so."

"And they expected to—to conquer us," Jessiss said, in a calm, faraway voice. "To wipe us out."

"Well—" I started.

"Human beings," Jessiss said. "They are, truly, most remarkably optimistic." And she giggled.

It was the giggle that did it. She'd given me the Hell of a last word.

I just nodded—letting her have it. Topping it was, just then, beyond human capacity.